A PLACE TO LIVE

Rebecca:
Happy Holidays!!

Abbi Weber

ABBI WEBER

ISBN 978-1-68526-825-1 (Paperback)
ISBN 978-1-68526-826-8 (Digital)

First Edition

Covenant Books
11661 Hwy 707
Murrells Inlet, SC 29576
www.covenantbooks.com

CHAPTER 1

"Ginnie, dear, did you know?"

"I suspected, but I wanted to be sure before I spoke to you," replied Minnie's best friend and sister-in-law. "I didn't know whether she was a client of George or a business associate."

"How did you find out?" asked Minnie.

"I saw George and Carole having lunch together at the food court in the mall while I was shopping. I thought it strange their eating lunch at three in the afternoon but didn't speak to them. They didn't know I had seen them. I just sat in the corner, having my cup of tea, watching. I thought it strange the way they were talking. Business associates sit up straight, looking at one another, watching one another to make sure the other person is being honest. George and Carole were leaning toward each other, their heads together, like lovers."

"How long ago was this?"

"Only a few days before George collapsed," replied Ginnie. "By then, it was unimportant, so I remained quiet. I had no information there was anything to it but an innocent business lunch. And I didn't want to hurt you more than you had already been hurt by George's dying."

"Yes," replied Minnie, "that's understandable. There was nothing in George's daily actions to make me suspect him of being unfaithful. Not until we and Blake reviewed George's business and personal papers. And afterward, at George's office, everything became too painfully clear."

"I'm so sorry, Minnie," Ginnie said. "Is there anything I can do for you?"

"Just knowing you're here for me, dear, and knowing I can depend on you for moral support. There's just the two of us against the world now. The only good thing to come of what has happened in the last week is you and I still have each other."

"Always, friends forever," replied Ginnie. "Whatever I can do to help, you just let me know."

The two women, lifelong friends, held hands. Eyes welling up with tears, they settled onto the bench close to the flower garden on the patio. They sat in silence, each lost in their own thoughts while the last streams of late summer sunlight drifted westward.

*****

There really wasn't anything to say. George was gone; George was the reason they were crying. They cried for George, of course, because he was gone and because of the mess he had made of his life and theirs and because they had no idea how they were going to right the mess caused by George. And they cried for themselves, the two of them, these two women who had been friends their entire adult lives, Ginnie and Minnie. They cried in fear for what was going to become of them now George was gone.

George had taken care of both of them, his sister, Ginnie, since she was a young girl, and Minnie for forty years of marriage. That was a lot of taking care of. He had never asked for help, just assumed it was his duty as brother and husband. After all, women needed a man to take care of them, go to work to earn money to pay the bills for the myriad necessities women had, manage the mortgage payment and accompanying bills, buy the groceries, handle the upkeep on the house, all those things. Everyone knew women couldn't handle those things by themselves; their minds just didn't work that way. What had Minnie's father told her? Sending women to college was a waste of time and money. Women had little intelligence to understand studies at the college level; they stayed home, got married, and took care of the house and children. Men go to work and earn the money to pay the bills. Working women take jobs away from men who need to work to feed their families. Besides, everyone knew if a woman landed a decent job, it was because she had slept with the boss in order to get the job in the first place. And he had meant it; that's the way it was in Bryant Hills in 1978.

But this was 2020, and George was gone. Try as she might, even though it was over forty years later and women had been acclimated into the workplace for more years than had passed since Minnie's father had admonished her for wanting to go to college. Minnie had no way of even knowing how to get a job, much less, perform the tasks needed to hold it. Who would hire a sixty-two-year-old woman who had never held a job a day in her life?

Minnie had always depended on George to earn the money to take care of their needs. Even while finishing college, George had worked eight hours a day in a grocery store from early afternoons to closing after attending his classes in the morning. George had earned the money to pay the rent, the heat and light bills, and the groceries. Minnie had taken care of their small apartment, did the weekly laundry, and cooked their meals. She'd taken a night class here and there for such things as flower arranging or gourmet cooking, had joined a book club or two, and had even taken a two-day course to learn how to operate their home computer. But she'd never been responsible for any of the money matters their lifestyle required. Now, forty years later, never going to college, never learning how to budget her household finances or how to manage any of the other bills was going to be her downfall. Now George was gone, and Minnie, along with Ginnie, was broke.

CHAPTER 2

Virginia Gardiner and Minerva Halbert had been friends since high school. But it wasn't until the last day of the second semester when they met. It was 1978; they were both eighteen years old, preparing to graduate from Bryant Hills High School. The spring air was tense with excitement in the school gymnasium as the graduation caps and gowns were being passed out to the high school seniors. The yearbooks had been distributed a couple of days before, and now everyone was running back and forth, trying on mortarboards and asking everyone else to sign their yearbooks. One-liners like "Wishing you all the luck in the world," "You're the best," or "We didn't have many classes together, but I know you'll be great someday" were scribbled next to individual photos or team pictures. Longer diatribes from BFFs took more time and space, generally written during study hall or lunch break—these had been collected first.

Ginnie and Minnie didn't travel in the same circles. While Ginnie was an A+ student, focusing on getting into the university and eventually becoming a writer, Minnie was part of the popular set. Minnie's time was occupied with captaining the cheerleading squad for the football, basketball, and baseball teams; dating jocks; making sure she wore the coolest clothes; and, oh yes—dating jocks.

Ginnie and Minnie had attended four years of high school in a small town, with only sixty-five students in the senior class, but had never spoken a word to each other. Ginnie had collected her gown and mortarboard, asked a few people to sign her yearbook, and was on her way out of the gymnasium. Minnie, as usual, was late. She had spent too much time in the girls' lavatory combing her long blonde hair into a ponytail and applying makeup. By the time she had completed her makeup, Minnie had to recomb her hair because the ponytail just didn't look right. By then, she should have been in the gym over an hour ago to collect her cap and gown. So she was rushing, rushing into the gymnasium when Ginnie was leaving—one pulling, the other pushing on the huge, heavy metal doors. Crash! Both girls were unceremoniously thrown onto the floor, on their bums!

CHAPTER 3

The heavy metal gymnasium double doors had been built so both doors opened toward a person when going in and opened out when leaving. But the mechanism controlling the doors had failed. As Ginnie was pushing on the door handle and Minnie was pulling on it, the equipment had buckled and then collapsed before opening toward Minnie but jolting Ginnie forward at the same time. In the confusion, both girls were literally knocked off their feet.

Sounds of their classmates giggling or oohing at their predicament came to Ginnie and Minnie as they hazily found themselves on the floor. Textbooks, the yearbook, purses, items from their pockets had been thrown down as well; lipsticks and pens rolling away from them across the floor. Together, quickly, to avoid as much embarrassment as possible, the girls began to pick themselves up, along with their belongings.

Even though Minnie was used to getting what she wanted most of the time, she wasn't completely shallow; clearly, she felt responsible for the accident. If she wouldn't have dawdled so long in the lavatory, this wouldn't have happened. Minnie got to her feet as quickly as she could and extended a hand to help Ginnie get up and to collect the items she had been carrying. As Ginnie started to boost herself up, she pushed with her right hand on the floor, uttering, "Oh-h-h!" and then a louder "Ouch! Dang, I've hurt my wrist."

The principal, Mr. Woods, was at the doorway in a second. After a few quick questions, he sent Minnie on her way to get her cap and gown and shepherded Ginnie to his office where she could sit down. He gingerly felt the bones in Ginnie's wrist and then telephoned her mother about the accident. To make a long story short, Ginnie graduated the next day with her sprained wrist bandaged in white and her right arm in a sling.

The following day after graduation, Minnie guiltily called Ginnie to see how she was doing. Ginnie confessed she was being very lazy—she hadn't done any of the household chores her mother expected her to do, because of the twinges of pain in her wrist. "What chores?" Minnie asked incredulously. Minnie had never been expected to do any chores in her own home. Her mother cooked and tidied up daily, but there was usually a local woman who came in on a weekly basis to do the heavy cleaning and laundry.

Ginnie explained her mother was a nurse working rotating shifts, sometimes at night, from midnight to 8:00 a.m. When working the midnight shift, Ginnie's mom slept during the day; and Ginnie was expected to make the beds, tidy up the bathroom, and put together a light lunch for herself and her brother, George. Some days, Ginnie was required to begin preparation for their evening meal by putting an entrée into the oven a couple of hours before her mother awoke and her father came home. When her mother worked the night shift, Ginnie sometimes made eggs and toast, or even pancakes, for herself and George for breakfast.

Minnie marveled at Ginnie's expertise in housekeeping and cooking. Once again, because she felt responsible for Ginnie's injury, Minnie volunteered to come over and help Ginnie with her daily chores.

From then on, it was BFF—best friends forever. Wherever one of the girls was, the other was sure to be there as well.

CHAPTER 4

A few weeks after both girls graduated from Bryant Hills High School, even though Ginnie's wrist was healing nicely, Minnie continued to help Ginnie with her daily housework. The two girls would breeze through the chores so they could spend more time talking with friends, window-shopping at the mall, or cooling off in the lake at the south side of the city. One morning, Minnie arrived at Ginnie's house earlier than usual. As Minnie opened the door, Ginnie's brother, George, was just going out. No one ended up on the floor this time, but both George and Minnie did a double take. George literally stopped in his tracks. Minnie halted as well. Minnie knew George was home from college for the summer; but until this morning, they hadn't met. Minnie knew George was tall, husky, a football player, and the pride of Ginnie's family. But Minnie hadn't known George was built like a Greek god and blessed with extraordinary good looks as well!

While Minnie was drooling over George's good looks and physique, George was blinded by Minnie's beautiful features, blonde hair, and movie-star figure. George had heard his sister talking about Minnie to their mother. He knew Minnie was captain of the cheerleading squad while in high school, knew all the "right people," and dated jocks, but as a friend to Ginnie, eagerly helped her with the daily household chores. He liked that. He could see Minnie wasn't just a social butterfly.

"Whoa," said George as they almost collided in the doorway.

Laughing, Minnie recovered first. "Oh, hi, you must be George, Ginnie's brother."

"Yeah, that's me," replied George, "and you must be Minnie Halbert."

That was the beginning of Minnie's forty-year love affair with George Gardiner. They dated during the summer and exchanged letters with each other when he was attending state college in Capitol City, and when George returned home the following summer, they decided to get married.

George's parents were good people. His mother was an experienced cancer care nurse. His father was an employee for a plumbing firm, installing and repairing fixtures; he could fix anything. Although George and Minnie's parents didn't meet socially, they knew each other; it was a small town. Minnie's parents knew George's family and readily accepted them as in-laws. Within three weeks, their mothers organized a small, intimate wedding to take place at the church rectory followed by a reception at Minnie's parents' home, attended by their immediate families with a few close friends of the parents and the bride and groom. George took a job at a supermarket in Capitol City and rented a small apartment for them there to be able to finish his final year of college. His major was business and finance, and he planned to go into investment banking after graduation; he dreamed of making it big while guiding his clients through the stock market!

But fate stepped in to interrupt the two lovebirds. During George's final year at college, his father was suddenly killed in a car accident. A winter storm bringing rain and then turning to ice and snow had made the roads quite treacherous; and while driving home from work, Mr. Gardiner swerved to stay clear of an oncoming car that had gone out of control, launching his vehicle into a steep ditch. The front end of his vehicle smashed into the ditch, and he was killed instantly.

George left college in the middle of his final year, and he and Minnie moved back to Bryant Hills. Even though his mother was an excellent nurse, her income wasn't enough to support herself and afford her to be able to pay for George's remaining semester or for Ginnie's college tuition as well. Ginnie had also begun attending the college in Capitol City, pursuing the writing career she had always wanted.

A small investment firm took George on as a clerk, and Ginnie was hired by the local newspaper as a setup typist. Minnie stayed at home, handling the housework, while George, Ginnie, and their mother pooled their salaries to help pay the monthly bills.

Minnie's father had often tried to help with the Gardiner finances, but George wouldn't have it. George always said he would never be able to repay Minnie's father and he wouldn't be owing to anyone for something he could do himself with a little hard work.

And work hard was exactly what George did. Within five years of starting as a clerk, George had risen to broker status in the investment firm. His acumen at choosing the best stocks for investment was incredulous. He had kept in touch with many of his college friends and listened when they talked; changes in electronics technology and medical technology were advancing rapidly, changing the world practically overnight. And George watched the companies making the biggest changes: IBM, Microsoft, Hewlett-Packard, Johnson & Johnson, Pfizer. He advised his clients to invest, and to invest big. Many of his clients were friends of his wife's father, who had mentioned his son-in-law's name in passing when discussing money. So after ten years in the investment business, eventually George opened his own office. Nothing as big or pretentious as the firm he had left but just enough to make a profit so he could continue to support his family.

By the time George's mother died, he had become so successful he decided to move his little family (himself, Minnie, and Ginnie) into a larger, more affluent home. Minnie's father was so proud of his son-in-law's success he purchased a beautiful two-story manor home with outbuildings and land in the same residential district where he and Minnie's mother lived. As a final protective gesture for his daughter, Mr. Halbert had put the house in Minnie's name, Minerva Gardiner, so she would always have a place to live.

But Minnie felt slighted; even though her father had put the title to the house in her name, he gave the papers for the house to George, saying, "Look after this for her, won't you, George?" Again, as a way of saying women could not handle money matters.

To George, it meant one thing: he had made it! He had arrived!

George, Minnie, and Ginnie lived in the big house, happy to be with each other. George and Minnie never had children, much to their regret; but they enjoyed having friends over for dinner, traveling from time to time, and sharing their beautiful home together.

Then one evening, while George was entertaining a business client in one of Bryant Hill's trendy restaurants, he spotted a lovely young woman at the end of the bar. She looked so forlorn, lonely, helpless. After his client left, he decided to ask the young woman if he could help with whatever was the problem. The woman was Carole Cameron, and she had just been let go from her position as administrative assistant. She was so strikingly beautiful and so upset. After they shared a couple of drinks, he decided to hire her on the spot. And so, Carole Cameron became George's secretary, not because George needed an administrative assistant but because Carole needed a job.

Within a few short months, the relationship developed into so much more. Somehow, Carole hadn't been able to pay her rent; somehow, Carole didn't like her apartment and wanted a nicer place in a more upscale neighborhood; somehow, Carole needed new clothes to present a more professional atmosphere in the office; and somehow, Carole had fallen in love with George, and George needed to spend an occasional night at Carole's apartment.

George didn't realize he had been wanting more out of his marriage to Minnie. After Minnie went through her menopause, the sex dwindled down to practically nothing. Minnie never noticed that even though she no longer cared for the pleasures of lovemaking, George did. Secretly, George considered joining a Gentlemen's Club to avail himself of an occasional lady's charms, but in the end, he couldn't betray Minnie in that way—it seemed too sordid. When he met Carole and hired her to work in his office, he was surprised to discover he had inadvertently made a woman available to himself. When Carole announced she had fallen in love with him, he didn't hesitate and readily jumped into the relationship.

When it began, the sex with Carole, George felt renewed. He hadn't taken part in such lovemaking for quite some time. Holding this vibrant, beautiful woman in his arms revitalized him like no magic elixir could return him to his youthful, more sexually active days. When Carole needed those little specialties like diamond earrings or that cute little sports car, George acquiesced, finding the funds from somewhere to be able to afford whatever it was Carole wanted. Carole had made it clear: if George *wouldn't* buy those things for her, well then, she would just pay a little visit to Minnie Gardiner!

Suddenly, George was in deep—too deep! He needed an outlet, something to relieve all the stress of keeping Carole hidden from Minnie, robbing his personal accounts to pay for the little luxuries Carole needed so badly, and trying to manage his client account base as successfully as he had always done.

The outlet came in the form of a casino in Capitol City. He and Carole had stayed in the casino hotel for a weekend's entertainment, gambling, swimming, dining. One morning, while Carole was enjoying a massage in the spa, George played poker in the high-stakes area of the casino. And he won big—35, as in thirty-five thousand dollars! After that, George and Carole began leaving the office early on Friday afternoons going to the casino in Capitol City. He began to tell Minnie he would be meeting a potential client for dinner to mask what he was doing with Carole on the weekends.

But he never again won an amount equal to the first big jackpot. By the time Ginnie spotted George and Carole having lunch at the food court of the local mall, George had not only gotten himself in deeper than before—he was also buried in debt!

First had come borrowing from his life insurance and then borrowing from Minnie's life insurance, followed with prematurely drawing money from his retirement fund. Finally, all his profits from his investment portfolio had disappeared. Everything—up in smoke! And the reason he and Carole were at the mall for lunch was because the midweek business buffet at the local hotel was too expensive. Carole was telling George she needed more new clothes and how her apartment wasn't working out for her. She felt she should move into one of those smart new condos down by the lake—oh, on and on about want she wanted… It just didn't end.

What Ginnie didn't see took place after she had finished her tea and continued her shopping. That was when George told Carole she could not have new clothes or the condo. She could not have anything anymore. She could begin looking for another job because he had just decided he had no need for an administrative assistant. There wasn't anything to administrate anymore. She was fired!

This news hit Carole like a ton of bricks. She stormed out of the food court, shouting after herself, "Well, we will just see what Mrs. Gardiner has to say about this!"

George returned home, spent a quiet night with his wife and sister, and went to bed early. The next day, he did not go to work, feigning being too tired and needing a day off. Carole didn't have access to Minnie's cell number, but George apprehensively listened throughout the day for the doorbell to ring. The following day, he called a business associate and invited him to a round of golf and lunch at the local golf course; and then, after scoring six on a simple Par 3, George went to retrieve his ball from the cup, leaned too far forward, fell onto his knees, then fell onto the green, and died.

CHAPTER 5

Blake Harrison was known as a "stand-up guy." At sixty-three years of age, he practiced family law throughout Bryant Hills and the surrounding towns, including a few lucrative clients in Capitol City. Wills, adoptions, and financial gifting were his specialties; but occasionally he dabbled in financial planning, especially for clients who wanted to ensure their proceeds were going to a specific beneficiary.

And he wasn't hard to look at either! Six feet four, sandy-brown hair with no hint of gray, soft green eyes, and a football quarterback's physique that had broadened only a little over the years. And he was a bachelor. This, along with his pleasant manner and unassuming personality, made him an excellent choice for dinner parties when an extra male was needed.

George had consulted Blake on occasion, especially in those early years when his business began to become successful, and George felt more financially secure to be able to afford such luxuries as life insurance. Blake had given him the name of a reputable agent and then recommended himself to draft wills for George and Minnie. It was at that time George put his retirement plan into his sister, Virginia's, name. Minnie's house, of course, was free and clear since her father had paid for it when he gave it to her. George felt with the proceeds from his investment portfolio and one-million-dollars' life insurance, Minnie would be well situated. He had always taken care of his sister. She deserved something too. In this way, both women would be looked after, after he was gone.

George and Blake continued their professional and social relationships through the years. George had always told Minnie, "If anything ever happens to me, call Blake immediately."

The morning George collapsed on the golf course, Minnie received the call from the local Bryant Hills police telling her George had just been rushed to the hospital. The policewoman making the call did not tell Minnie George had died on the green of the sixth hole—she left that unpleasant task for the doctor. Minnie rushed to the hospital to be met in the doorway by their family practitioner who gave her the sad news. The next few hours were a blur of identifying George, getting his body released to the morgue for an autopsy, contacting a mortician to begin preparations for the funeral, and signing releases for the myriad things to be done. By the time Minnie was able to go home, she was distraught, confused and so deep in shock she could barely move. Then, remembering what George had always told her, she called Blake Harrison.

Blake immediately met Minnie at her home. He contacted Ginnie at the newspaper, requesting she quickly come home. After telling Ginnie about her brother's death, he sat both women in the sunroom and slipped into the kitchen to put on a pot of coffee. He then phoned their minister and requested he come to the home as well; both women would need his spiritual help and comfort. Blake stayed into the early evening, making sandwiches to sustain both the women, the minister, and himself. Before leaving, he set an appointment for Minnie and Ginnie to be in his office at one o'clock the next afternoon to review George's personal affairs.

And so, on a clear, warm late summer afternoon, Minnie and Ginnie arrived at Blake Harrison's office at 1:00 p.m. Blake greeted them warmly, having known them socially for many years, offered coffee or tea, and informed the women the insurance agent George had consulted would be in the meeting as well. Following introductions, Blake opened the portfolio containing the final information for George and Minerva Gardiner and Virginia Gardiner. But the information to be given was not what the women had expected. Blake and the insurance consultant steeled themselves for a difficult task: they had to tell the women there was almost nothing left of an estate that originally was worth close to two million dollars!

George's investment portfolio had completely disappeared, his life insurance was just enough to cover his funeral expenses, Minnie's life insurance was nonexistent, and there was no retirement income for Ginnie. Blake and the insurance consultant sat quietly, patiently waiting for the women to absorb what the two men had just said. Minnie looked exactly as she had the previous evening, in shock. Ginnie recovered first and said, "But George said he would always take care of me. I was to receive the proceeds from a retirement fund he initiated just for me. It was in my name."

Blake had to tell her, "You are not the beneficiary of that fund."

"Who is?" asked Ginnie in utter disbelief.

"That is confidential information," replied Blake.

Ginnie persisted, "You must tell me. Who is the beneficiary?"

Blake was adamant. "I'm sorry, it's my job to keep confidential information—confidential."

In the end, Ginnie realized it would be futile to pursue the matter; she could see losing the retirement fund George had always said would be hers was too upsetting for Minnie, as if losing his insurance benefits and investments wasn't enough. She had heard Minnie crying through the night following the disastrous day she had experienced yesterday. Ginnie wasn't feeling much better than Minnie, but she felt it was her duty to help Minnie through this terrible time and pulled herself together.

The insurance consultant took his leave, and Blake reviewed their financial situation as it was so they would know what to expect for monthly bills and responsibilities. He began by saying Minnie was the sole inheritor of George's possessions: their house, the remainder of his business income, all their household furnishings, etc. George received social security benefits which arrived on the second Wednesday of each month. Although George received monthly dividends from his clients' investments, it would be approximately thirty to ninety days before the final check would appear. Then George's accounts would be given to another investment professional to monitor. The social security served as income, and he wanted to start on a positive note.

What came afterward was completely negative. The savings account George shared with Minnie was down to nil; their checking account held a mere thirty dollars. Monthly bills included a mortgage payment, insurance on the house and cars and George's Medicare supplement policy, car loans on George's Mercedes and Minnie's Buick, utilities (gas, electric, water, garbage), telephone, television, internet, groceries, gas for the two cars, haircuts, spa treatments, and other incidentals.

"Hold it," Minnie interjected. "How am I supposed to pay all of those bills every month with just what I receive from social security? I've never had to pay bills before, but even I know social security won't stretch that far. And what am I to do about funeral expenses? And where did all our money go?"

It was as though Minnie had awakened from a dream. The dream had begun yesterday morning with the phone call from the local police and continued through the night and almost this entire day. She had endured the barrage of information given to her from Blake and the insurance consultant. She felt as though she was in some weird movie with everyone pulling a scam; they would eventually say, "April Fool!" and begin to quote what she could expect to receive from George's business income and insurance. Surely George had engaged someone to handle all this for her. She had known Blake for years. He was a regular at her dinner parties. Why was he doing this to her?

The lawyer spoke evenly. "I've prepared a few ideas for you to consider. I'm sorry, I cannot tell you where the money went, but it *is* gone. I realize this is extremely difficult for you to grasp. I didn't discover what had happened until this morning when I spoke with the insurance consultant. It is as much a surprise for me as it is for you, Minnie. I'm trying to soften as many blows for you as I can."

Blake offered the ladies another cup of coffee and suggested they take a small recess to freshen up, perhaps relax for a few minutes before they continued.

Minnie felt terrible about her outburst; she had never spoken to anyone in that tone of voice ever before. Ginnie felt Minnie was justified with what she had said but kept her thoughts to herself. Later, she would speak to Minnie about it when they were alone.

Fifteen minutes later, the ladies agreed to discuss ways to acquire money to be able to afford their way of life. Blake began by suggesting George's funeral need not be an elaborate affair. Cremation was widely accepted and more economical than a service with an elegant casket, burial site at the cemetery, and a huge reception to include everyone in a small town. There was a modest but adequate amount remaining from George's life insurance policy (after taxes, of course) for his funeral. It was Minnie's prerogative to arrange George's funeral whatever way she preferred. The funeral home could explain what needed to be done for the cremation and death certificate; the cost would include the urn, the services, flowers, and death announcements. Minnie was not obligated to host a huge reception with food and refreshments. If she wanted to have a few close friends at her home following the ceremony, she could do so by invitation.

Minnie had never considered what she would do if it became necessary to organize a funeral for her husband. Death was never something she ever thought about; she always felt she and George would grow old together. Hearing Blake explain how to present a proper funeral for her husband without overspending now, after she had discovered there were no funds available, she agreed cremation and the service at the funeral home was enough. After all, George had let her down; she was truly broke and on her own. Even though she still loved George, she hated him for putting her into this position.

Blake offered to go with Minnie to the funeral home the following morning to make the arrangements for George's last rites.

How to give George a proper funeral without putting Minnie into bankruptcy had been Blake's priority. Now that was decided, he presented two options to Minnie and Ginnie to gain income. Minnie now owned two vehicles, one of them a luxury item. It was impossible to drive two vehicles at the same time. Blake suggested Minnie sell George's Mercedes. There were two more years of payments required, but a good price could still be gotten for it. Minnie could pay off the loan and put the remainder toward her bills. She should be able to clear two months of mortgage payments for her home. Another suggestion was Ginnie's car, a sensible Chevrolet two-door, free and clear of any loan encumbrance. If the two women agreed they could get along with the use of just one vehicle, Minnie's Buick could also be sold. The women thought this was an excellent suggestion, and they would discuss it as soon as time allowed.

Blake had considered suggesting Minnie sell her lovely manor home and grounds. However, there was still a mortgage on the home. Should a good price be obtained for the property, the remainder of the mortgage would need to be deducted from the proceeds of the sale; and after seeing and hearing how distraught Minnie became following George's death and the review of his financial portfolio, he decided against it. Despite the funds the sale would make available to Minnie, the necessity of living *somewhere* would still exist. Earlier that morning, he had brainstormed options with the insurance consultant. The consultant suggested Minnie and Ginnie speak with a friend of his who specialized in reverse mortgages. Blake would suggest this idea to the ladies over the next few days as well as proposing he and the insurance consultant would accompany them to visit with the reverse mortgage agent.

Blake had other ideas as to how to increase the ladies' income, but he felt he had done enough for one day. Minnie and Ginnie were exhausted and wanted to be on their way. Minnie agreed to meet Blake at the local funeral home the following morning at ten and, courteous as ever, thanked him for his help and then left his office.

Ginnie had driven them to Blake's office in her car because Minnie felt she was unable to concentrate on driving through the afternoon traffic. But as they began driving again, Minnie said she wanted to stop at George's office to see what she needed to do to clear out his files and important papers. They drove to the downtown section of Bryant Hills. For thirty years, George had worked in the building next to a hardware store. It was three stories tall, with several offices on the first floor and a side stairway leading to second- and third-floor rental apartments. The ladies walked down the inside corridor leading to the office with George's name and "Investment

Consultant" written on the door. Minnie drew the key from her purse and began to insert it into the lock. Then she noticed the door was unlocked, partially open, and someone was rummaging about inside!

CHAPTER 6

Minnie and Ginnie expected to see a burglar with a mask covering his eyes and holding a gun as he dug through the file drawers looking for…what? Instead, they were relieved to encounter a very shapely young woman sorting through George's business papers and stacking files into boxes. The latter had not heard the two women coming into the office and approaching her. She muttered to herself while she worked—words sounding like "Now where did he put that?" and "I thought that was in this file."

Minnie cleared her throat and said, "A-hem! Is there something we can help you with?" The young woman straightened and turned to face them with a jolt. "Oh no. I was just doing some filing. I'm Mr. Gardiner's associate. Is there anything I can help *you* with?"

"As far as I knew," Minnie responded, "Mr. Gardiner didn't have a partner or an associate."

"Well," the woman replied, "I've been working for Mr. Gardiner for almost two years. It must be quite some time since you were here last."

"No," Minnie countered, "my husband never spoke of having a secretary or a partner."

"Your husband?" The woman spoke apprehensively. "You must be Mrs. Gardiner. I'm happy to meet you. My name is Carole Cameron."

Minnie felt there was something terribly wrong finding this young woman in George's office, and the look on her sister-in-law's face told her Ginnie felt the same. "What are you doing here?" Minnie now asked in her best authoritative voice.

The woman answered, "Truth be told, I gave my notice to Mr. Gardiner last week. But in lieu of what happened this week, I felt it was only decent of me to sort through and pack up George—I mean Mr. Gardiner's—business papers and client files. I thought you'd appreciate..."

"Stop right there," Minnie commanded. "If you are no longer an employee in this office, you have no right to be here. This information is now *my* personal property."

"Yes, well, some of these papers belong to me," the young woman responded precociously, "especially the claim form for his retirement income." She continued in a flirtatious manner, saying, "You see, George and I were an item. He owes me for 'services rendered,' if you know what I mean."

"Really?" said Minnie. "Just how much would his retirement income be? And what were you planning to do with these boxes of information about his clients? Sell them to the highest bidder?"

"Don't get tough with me, lady," the woman answered. "I have no qualms telling this whole town what George Gardiner was doing with his secretary in Capitol City while he was supposed to be wining and dining potential clients."

"Go ahead," countered Minnie, "and I'll report you to the investment companies George represented so they can levy a fraud charge against you."

"Give me my fifty-eight thousand, and I'm out of here," said Carole in an extremely surly tone. "I'm tired of pretending I enjoy making love with old goats."

Minnie's anger had reached its peak; everything that had happened in the last two days now seemed to come in on her. The shock of George dying, having to make decisions at the hospital with no one to help, the humiliation of learning George had left her and Ginnie broke, and finally, the audacity of this woman who most certainly was the reason for her being broke—everything Minerva Halbert Gardiner had ever endured was rolled into this situation. "Ms. Cameron," Minnie shouted at Carole as her anger rose, "that 'old goat' to whom you are referring was my husband, whether you cared for him or not. Take your filthy fifty-eight thousand in whore money and leave. Now!"

CHAPTER 7

"Oh, Minnie, you were spectacular," Ginnie congratulated her sister-in-law and friend. "I have never seen you so authoritative. Thank you, thank you for rescuing George's dignity."

Minnie was shaking like a leaf in a strong wind. Twice in the same day, she had vented her feelings to another person. But this time, she truly had taken another person to task and shown her the door. "Well," she said in a still-trembling voice, "now we know where all the money went including what happened to your retirement account."

Together, the two women restored the files and papers to their appropriate file drawers and then, after being careful to note the appearance of the office, locked the doors and walked to Ginnie's car. Minnie would tell Blake Harrison about her encounter with the famous Ms. Cameron in the morning and ask if he could contact the investment company's home office to inform them of George's passing so they could arrange for another agent to manage the clients. It would also be helpful if Blake could contact the building owner to let them know the office would be vacant for a few days until a new agent could replace George. She intended to contact the new agent herself to request George's personal files be boxed and delivered to her home.

It was late, after six o'clock, by the time the women arrived home. At Ginnie's insistence, sensing Minnie was as hungry as she, they stopped to pick up fish and chips for supper. As the women ate the food, they discussed the events of their day. It was clear they needed to put George to rest before they made any further decisions, even if those decisions were about money. Blake Harrison would help them navigate the arrangements for the funeral, the sale of one or both of Minnie's vehicles, and whatever could be done about the home mortgage.

Following supper, Minnie and Ginnie tidied the kitchen, put on a pot of tea, and sat next to each other on the patio of Minnie's beautiful home, wondering what was to become of them.

CHAPTER 8

The funeral for George Patrick Gardiner—native of Bryant Falls, lived there all his life, well-known in social circles, investment consultant, husband, brother, football star when in high school—was a quiet affair. As Blake Harrison suggested to Minnie, George was cremated. There was a viewing with pictures, flowers, and noted certificates of achievements with a brief ceremony at the funeral home for three hours on a Tuesday afternoon; but that was the extent of the public service. Minnie and Ginnie hosted a reception by invitation only for a few of their and George's closest friends and business associates. The group numbered about twenty individuals, and the two women made and served the food.

Not a very grand send-off into the hereafter for a man who, according to everyone, was known as a friendly, hardworking, intelligent person with an acumen for investing that enabled many in Bryant Hills to become more than modestly comfortable with their finances. That George had squandered not just every nickel he earned but had also put his wife and sister on the brink of bankruptcy was not made public. Blake and the insurance agent managed their client base as doctors do; any information was considered confidential. By the time they reached the afternoon of the funeral, both women felt betrayed beyond words. They were polite and cordial to their guests, accepting condolence and sympathy wishes with grace. But that was the extent of their grieving; now their grief became utter disbelief.

Blake Harrison, a friend to Minnie and Ginnie for many years, suddenly became invaluable. Using the resources at his disposal, he secured the proper forms to claim the remainder of the money left in the insurance policies. It wasn't much, but at least Minnie wouldn't owe for the cost of the cremation and funeral for George. The mortgage, car payments, country club dues and tabs, and the household bills had been paid for the month; but in two weeks, they would all be due again; and neither Minnie nor Ginnie had the funds to cover them.

Blake used the local and Capitol City newspapers to advertise the Mercedes for sale. For now, Minnie would keep her Buick. The hope was the Mercedes would sell for a good price enabling Minnie to pay off both vehicles and still make a little money on the deal. There were other places to cut expenses. Minnie agreed to drop the country club membership (she wasn't going to be having lunch there anytime soon); frequenting the spa for a massage, facial, and having her nails done was also now out of the question; and haircuts could be gotten much cheaper at the barber college than at an expensive salon. What Minnie insisted on was having Leona Potter, a local cleaning woman, help with the heavy cleaning twice a month. Leona needed the income from her work. She was a widow like Minnie, trying to keep her head above water.

Eliminating luxuries wasn't as painful for Minnie as she had thought it would be. She did not want to see any of her friends from the country club right now. The women she associated with at the country club had nothing better to do than gossip about other people, especially women in the surrounding area. Minnie knew she would be their "hot topic" this week and for weeks to come. Regardless of his downfall, Minnie had a good life with George and over the years became protective of their private affairs. She felt what had happened to her was no one's business but her own.

She and Ginnie would find a way out of this mess.

Despite the hurt Minnie felt from what George had done, she went through the days after his death and funeral thinking something else was going to happen. It was like waiting for the other shoe to drop, but she couldn't put a finger on what it could be. The nagging feeling continued until two days after George's funeral when she, Ginnie, and Blake Harrison met with the banker who held the mortgage on her house. The lawyer had once again organized the meeting as he continued to try to take as much responsibility from the women as he could. It was all part of his personal service to his clients.

The banker began by expressing his sympathy to both women; but then he quickly quoted the amount of the original loan, the amount of the monthly payment, and the remaining amount that still needed to be paid. The banker was unaware neither Minnie nor Ginnie were to receive any insurance from George's death. Blake had not given the banker that information; he wanted to see what could be done with the mortgage without going into Minnie's finances. For now, the banker assumed the women would be well situated because George had been so successful with his investment firm and had always concentrated on taking care of his wife and sister.

On the other hand, Blake never knew the house solely belonged to Minnie. He didn't know her father had purchased the house and grounds for her when George became successful in his business. At the time, Minnie and George were married for about ten years, and this was her father's way of putting his final stamp of approval on George. It was also her father's way of protecting his daughter; no matter what happened, she would always have a place to live.

So when the banker began his litany of numbers, Minnie's head began to spin. Oh, dear, oh yes, this was what had been bothering her. Interrupting the banker, she spoke in a hesitant voice. "Excuse me, I have a question."

The banker patiently stopped talking. "Yes, Mrs. Gardiner, what can I help you with?" he asked.

"I understand the amount of the loan, the interest rate, and the amount of the monthly payment. But what I don't understand is why there *is* a loan. My house has always been *my* house. My father bought it for me thirty years ago so I would always have a place to live. Father may have given George the papers of the sale, but he gave me the title. The title is in my name only. How could anyone, even my husband, take out a loan against my house and property?"

The banker looked at Minnie dumbfoundedly. "What?" he exclaimed.

Now it was Minnie's turn as she patiently began her question again, but the banker stopped her midsentence.

"You hold the title, solely in your name?" he asked.

"Yes," replied Minnie, taking up her purse and opening it, "I have the title here. I brought it with because I thought you might be needing it. As you can see, it is in my name only, as my father stipulated when he purchased the house and grounds for me thirty years ago. Nothing is written in the section where the mortgage should be listed because my father paid for it in full before he gave it to me. It is free and clear. There is not, nor ever has been, a mortgage on my house."

To his credit, the banker recoiled and then rebounded quickly. He had never come across a situation as this, ever. He needed to do more extensive research than he had done prior to this meeting. It never occurred to him the title or ownership of the house and grounds of the Gardiner estate were in anyone else's name other than George Gardiner. He had assumed this matter could quickly be negotiated with the presentation of George's death certificate and Mrs. Gardiner would take over repayment of the loan. Suddenly, this simple matter was more than simple—it had become insurmountable. If what Mrs. Gardiner said was true, the negotiation of the loan for George Gardiner was illegal.

The only thing the banker could think of at this moment was the lawsuit there could be against his bank and himself—the person who approved the loan.

CHAPTER 9

Once again, it was Blake who had the presence of mind to suggest a break would be welcomed by everyone attending the meeting. The ladies left for the powder room, Blake busied himself refilling the coffee cups, and the banker dashed to the upper level of the building to confer with the loan officer who had originally drafted the documents for the loan to George Gardiner. It was some time before the banker returned to the meeting room. After seating himself, he spoke in a soft, careful tone.

"Mrs. Gardiner, Ms. Gardiner, please forgive me for taking such an extensive break. I wanted to be sure what I am telling you now is correct. After conferring with the officer who initiated the documents for the loan to your husband, Mrs. Gardiner, an error has been discovered. I'll need some time to research this matter more completely. Would it be possible for you, Ms. Gardiner, and Mr. Harrison to meet with me again, say, Thursday morning at 9:30?"

"What kind of error?" asked the ever-vigilant Blake Harrison.

"As far as I can tell, it looks like a clerical error," the banker answered.

"Ours or yours?" Blake persisted.

"The bank's," replied the banker.

Blake glanced at Minnie and Ginnie. Without a word, he could see the look of relief coming over their faces as they nodded in agreement to the banker's suggestion. "Yes," Blake said, "that is agreeable to us."

"Very well then, I shall look forward to meeting with you again on Thursday. Please, have a good day, until then."

The trio rose from their chairs and quietly walked out of the meeting room. When they were out of the building, in the parking lot, Blake quietly told the women to go home; he would call them within the hour. He needed some time to make a few calls of his own.

Forty-five minutes later, he called Minnie. She promptly put her cell phone onto the speaker setting so she and Ginnie could both hear what he had to say. "From what my sources tell me, we may have uncovered not just a clerical error but a huge discrepancy on the part of the bank and the loan officer. It was completely illegal for George to take a loan on property he did not own. Obviously, the loan officer assumed because George was your husband, Minnie, this meant you and he owned the house and property together. I had a friend of mine in real estate check the original title and documents that were drafted when your father made the purchase. The title is still in your name only Minnie. An educated guess tells me, after more extensive research is done by the bank, they may just forgive the loan, take the loss, and not require any further payments from you. Since George did make payments for the five years prior to his death, I feel you should be reimbursed for those payments on the grounds the loan was illegal from the start. I'm going to begin preparing papers to initiate a lawsuit against the bank and the person who approved this transaction without your knowledge if that doesn't happen."

The ladies could not believe what they were hearing. George had initially borrowed $250,000 against the value of Minnie's home and property. Even though he had made payments on the loan over the last five years, a substantial amount due remained. At this point, having the loan forgiven because the bank wanted to avoid a lawsuit sounded like a gift from heaven.

With no huge mortgage payment to make every month, the expenses on Minnie's house and property would be substantially decreased. The ladies spent the rest of the afternoon compiling what bills they would now be expected to pay.

But, coupled with the two car payments that still existed, the expected income fell appallingly short!

CHAPTER 10

Virginia Gardiner was a formidable woman in her own right. Although it seemed she was always behind the scenes, Ginnie had grown from the awkward teenager she was when she and Minnie met to a very capable woman. Quiet and shy in high school, she had few friends; and those friends were just like her—studious, unassuming, and working quietly to qualify for acceptance to a good college. The summer Ginnie spent with Minnie as her first close friend was fantastic. But when summer ended, Ginnie had to get down to work. She attended the university in Capitol City with her brother. Because she was a freshman, her studies were general requirements; the classes focusing on becoming a writer were not yet available to her. She was just beginning her second semester when her father lost his life on the icy road. Now it was decision time!

Her parents' dual income made it possible for both their children to attend college and stay in the dormitory. But when her father died, it was clear there was no way her mother could afford to send two children to college. George was already married to Minnie, and he was in his final year of studies. He should have the chance to finish. Ginnie realized she could always go back to school, taking night classes, to get her degree. Without telling her mother, Ginnie dropped out of college and secured a position at the local Bryant Hills newspaper as a setup typist. Her mother was disappointed but, due to the circumstances, welcomed the additional income.

Ginnie worked hard at the newspaper. In a span of forty-plus years, she had been promoted from setup typist to page layout to proofreader and currently as editor of the women's section. Receiving appropriate pay raises and benefits along the way, Ginnie had made herself one of the valued employees of the newspaper. And she had done it by herself, working from the bottom up, making friends and business associates along the way. She was well respected; other employees knew if they would go to her with questions, they would receive fair, knowledgeable answers. Even though Ginnie had never become a famous writer, she felt her career at the newspaper was very rewarding, and she had achieved a certain status among her peers.

While Minnie had boutique shops, spas, and the country club available to her, Ginnie preferred to buy her clothing and personal items at the more economical stores in Bryant Hills. Occasionally, for special events, Ginnie would splurge on a pretty dress or accessories; but for the most part, she was careful how she spent her money.

When Minnie's father purchased a beautiful house and property for her, Ginnie was overwhelmed when she was invited to share it with her sister-in-law and brother, granted it was big enough to house a small army; but she didn't want to intrude on the married couple's life. However, Minnie and George insisted she live with them. She could have her own private room and bath on the second floor, and the garage was big enough to allow for three vehicles—Ginnie was elated.

Beautiful was not the word for Minnie's house; fabulous, fantastic, gorgeous were better words. Facing south, to take advantage of the eastern, southern, and western sun during the day, the house and property sat on two full acres smack in the middle of the best residential district in Bryant Hills. In the old days, it had been part of a farm. The house was a huge, sturdy five-bedroom Tudor built in the late 1800s. There were two large windows flanking each side of the big wooden front door. After walking in, a generous living room leading to a dining room were to the right. From the living room, French doors opened to a spacious sunroom. A fireplace straddled the wall between the living and dining rooms so it could be seen from either side—a feature allowing both rooms to be kept cozy in wintertime.

To the left of the front door was a large foyer entryway with a stairway to the second floor. Farther left was the master bedroom with another fireplace, sitting area, and private bathroom. Behind the foyer and stairway was the kitchen. Two patio doors, a back door, and large window stretched across the back of the house. The upstairs held four bedrooms, two on each side of the house with a shared bathroom between each set of rooms; a snug encompassed the area along the back wall of the stairway.

The property behind the house held a patio, the garage, two smaller outbuildings, and a small kitchen garden surrounded with apple, plum, and maple trees. At the front of the house sat an ages-old weeping willow tree next to the driveway.

Through the years, Ginnie's promotions had been profitable to her. Living with Minnie and George in their beautiful home, Ginnie literally had no household expenses except an occasional car payment, clothing, hairdressing, and picking up a bagful of groceries now and then on her way home from work. Her car insurance was bundled with George and Minnie's to receive a better rate. Socking away a tidy sum every month was a piece of cake.

Now forty-some years later after becoming best friends forever with Minnie, Ginnie found herself offering Minnie a modest sum for monthly rent at a time when Minnie could certainly use the income. At first Minnie declined; she would find a way to make ends meet. George had always taken care of his sister; as George's wife, Minnie would continue to do so. But Ginnie was adamant. Minnie and her brother had always been so kind to her; helping now, even with money, was the least she could do especially since Minnie needed the help so badly. And so, after reviewing the money situation one more time, Minnie conceded. In the future, things would be sunnier (in the future, wouldn't they?), when Minnie's life would once again be on an even keel, and then Minnie would no longer accept Ginnie's rent payment.

It was a place to start. And right now, Minnie desperately needed a place to start.

CHAPTER 11

After the Gardiner women and Blake Harrison left the building, the banker rushed to his office. He could not believe what he had allowed to happen. He had been in the banking and mortgage business for twenty-five years, and he had never done anything such as this. How could he have been so absentminded to let this pass? He remembered the day he approved the loan for George Gardiner speculating why George would need extra money and why it would be needed so quickly. Surely, that was a private issue on George's part. He had the collateral to make the loan possible.

The banker had befriended George Gardiner during the years when George was struggling to make a success of his investment business. George was continually sending new clients to the bank; they needed a place to store the profits they were making from George's excellent investment advice. The banker had become so friendly with George he was occasionally invited to George's home for dinner parties.

But, the banker reasoned, he was not alone in this error. The loan officer who had drafted the initial documents also assumed, as a man, George owned his house and the grounds it sat on. This was a common conception. Why wouldn't a man own his house and grounds? Why would anyone think a man's house and grounds would be owned, solely, by his wife? Women didn't own any kind of property unless if they owned it jointly with their husband, didn't they? Yes, Minnie had come from a wealthy family, she had been an only child, but that wasn't any reason to think she alone would own a successful man's house—was it?

He could easily understand why the papers would have been drafted in George's name as owner of the property. It would have been a natural assumption. The officer ran a credit check on George as a matter of course; but in view of the business George sent to the bank, how successful he had become, and the current value of the house and property, making the loan was an easy business arrangement. No one, not even the banker, had inquired why the loan was needed. And everything fell into place so nicely, neither the loan officer nor the banker had taken the time to research the title or the original purchase of the land and house made by Minnie's father twenty-five years earlier.

So…learning the house and property was solely owned by Minerva Gardiner, George's wife, had been left undiscovered.

In the end, as the chief loan officer, the banker assumed the associate who had drafted the original documents had done the due diligence required to check out Mr. Gardiner's credit report among other things including the title on the property; and the loan officer assumed the same from the banker.

Reaching for his laptop, the banker quickly accessed the website available to businesses like banks, mortgage companies, realtors, tax assessors, etc. He punched in the appropriate coordinates and brought to the screen the title to the Gardiner house and property. Yup! There it was in black and white. Clearly written in the title section was "Minerva Mary Gardiner." No George and Minerva; no George Gardiner and Minerva Gardiner; no George in any way, shape, or form. Damn!

Then he accessed the original documents of the purchase of the house and property. Again, as Minerva Gardiner had said, clearly written in black and white was the name of her father, Thomas Halbert, as the purchaser, and the date of the sale in 1990.

He pressed the link to the loan documents drafted five years earlier for the loan given to George. In the collateral section was written "house." No value of the house given despite the current value was now more than three times what the house and property had been worth in 1990. The banker's signature was at the bottom in approval of the loan. The only other pertinent information on the form was George's social security number, his address, and his phone number. Good Lord! It was as though George had walked into the bank and said, "I need some money quick," and the bank, or rather he, as the banker, had turned it over to him.

Then he pressed another link providing mortgage information and found that blank as well. As Minerva Gardiner had said so emphatically in their meeting, "There is not, nor ever has been, a mortgage on my house." The woman was right!

Well, yes, she was right to a certain extent. There was no mortgage made on the house and property by Minnie's father or herself. But there was a personal loan taken by her husband, George. A loan approved by himself as the chief loan officer of the bank. A loan taken out illegally because the house was not owned by George Gardiner. No one at the bank had bothered to confirm George Gardiner did, in fact, own the property he had used as collateral for his personal loan.

Damn, damn, double damn!

He had to stop for a second; he had to think about this. What could be done? God, he wished he still smoked; this would be a perfect time to go outside the building. He had to clear his head and reason what he could do about this terrible error he had made. He closed the website, logged off his computer, and left the office. Telling the person at the front desk he would not be back again that day, he walked to his car and drove to the nearest bar.

*****

Two Rob Roys and almost an hour later, the banker had decided what to do. He had to make this right. He had mistakenly approved a loan using property for collateral whom the person taking the loan did not own. Regardless of whether Mrs. Gardiner already owned the house and property, regardless of whether Mr. and Mrs. Gardiner were married over forty years, and regardless of whether George Gardiner had shown his many clients to the bank over the years, the loan was still illegal. Mrs. Gardiner needed to be relieved of the loan payments as well as reimbursed for the payments her late husband had made over the last five years. This was the only avenue to take, and he *had* to make it happen.

Returning to the bank the following day, the banker logged on to his computer and this time accessed his own personal bank account. Working online, he withdrew two hundred thousand dollars plus and transferred it to the loan. After calculating the total payments George had made over the last five years and applying an additional current interest, he marked the account "Paid in Full" and closed it out. He would make a personal check to Mrs. Gardiner for the payments plus interest her husband had made. He would hold his breath as to how this had been handled and face whatever circumstances that came of this situation; after all, he was completely responsible for what had happened, and he needed to face that inevitably.

Thursday morning, when the two Gardiner women and Blake Harrison met once again in his office, he kept the explanation as simple as possible about what had happened. After all, he was talking to women. It had been a mistake. Mr. Gardiner had sent quite a bit of business to the bank over the years from his successful investment of his client's money. "It was logical," the banker said with a demeaning nod to Minnie, "for the bank to assume Mr. Gardiner owned the house and property where he lived because he was a man. In order to save time, because Mr. Gardiner insisted on receiving the funds as quickly as possible, the bank wrote the transaction as a personal loan instead of a mortgage. This was why the title had never needed updating."

And I never found out about the loan, Minnie mused. *What a clever way to keep something hidden from a spouse.* The banker profusely apologized to Minnie for any inconvenience she may have experienced and presented her with his personal check in reimbursement of the payments George had made plus interest.

Satisfied with the situation, Blake did not mention the lawsuit he was prepared to propose against the banker and his bank. The generous amount of the reimbursed loan payments enabled Minnie to pay her monthly bills without worry. He would discuss investment options with her at another time. For now, Minnie and Ginnie were safe.

But the meeting wasn't over yet. Once again, Minnie ventured, "Excuse me, but I have one more question."

The banker nodded at her to go ahead.

Minnie had never been an advocate for women's rights, or anyone else's rights, but she ventured, "If I would have come to you, a woman asking for a loan using my home and property as collateral, even with the title in my hand, how long would the bank take to investigate me before granting the loan? Would the bank have taken the time to do the due diligence, then?"

"Well, Mrs. Gardiner, that is a hypothetical question," was the reply as the banker wondered how a housewife would know about due diligence.

"Why?" Minnie asked. "Because women don't own houses or property by themselves?"

The banker remained quiet.

"Sir," Minnie continued in a chastising voice, "I thank you for returning the money you took from George for a bogus loan. But you should be aware—it is no longer the 1800s, nor is it the 1900s. This is 2020, and right now, there *is* a woman in front of you who has owned her home and the surrounding property for over thirty years."

With that, Minnie rose and left the bank, not looking behind her to see if Harrison and her sister-in-law were following.

When Ginnie reached the outside of the bank, she clenched her fist, pulled it toward her body, and said to Minnie, "You go, girl!"

CHAPTER 12

During the weeks following the funeral, Minnie slowly became acclimated to taking care of herself. With Ginnie's help and a few books from the library on budgeting, she created a payment schedule on her computer for each of the house bills, indicating the time of the month when the payments were due and an area to check as they were paid. Ginnie showed her how to balance her checkbook; another task Minnie had always left for George.

In the same folder, with a tab, she listed the activities or expenses she used to do with a note next to each when it could be eliminated from her daily routine. The majority of these items were the fun things she used to do to keep herself occupied during the day when her late husband was at work: playing golf, lunching with her friends, relaxing at the spa, having her hair or nails done at the salon, shopping, or preparing for her endless dinner parties.

It was obvious none of these activities would now be affordable. Upon reflection, it was amazing how coolly she had gone about her days as though she was the only person who mattered. How could she have been so thoughtless? Surprisingly, it was Ginnie she thought about, what must she have felt, while going to her job at the newspaper every day, seeing Minnie so fancy-free, depending solely on George to take care of all her needs.

Now there were tasks she had to do of greater importance: sell the Mercedes, pay off the Mercedes and her Buick, and sign the title for the vehicle over to the new owner; talk to the insurance agent about a new life policy for herself (Ginnie had life insurance through her employer); sort through the boxes of files from George's office;

and search for ways to increase her monthly income. Yes, the reimbursement from the illegal loan to George using her house and property as collateral was very generous. But if she relied on those funds to support herself, she would be penniless within three to four years. She could not rely on those funds alone.

Reflecting again at her ignorance of what George had been doing with their life insurance policies, the investment income he had built up over forty years, and Ginnie's retirement plan proceeds, she marveled at how it could have happened. Even if she wasn't there to stop George from robbing Peter to pay Paul, why didn't anyone else say something like "George, do you really want to cash out this insurance?" or "You do know, George, this will leave your wife and sister without an income if you suddenly pass away." Even Blake Harrison had not stepped in on her and Ginnie's behalf. How could he have let that happen? But then, she remembered Blake saying, at the first meeting they had following George's demise, he had just learned where her income had gone while talking with the insurance agent. Blake had been as surprised as she. The insurance agent, the person who monitored the retirement fund, even the banker—it wasn't their fault this had happened. Clearly, the fault was on her late husband. He had allowed himself to be swayed by a pretty face, and Minnie and Ginnie were suffering the consequences for his actions.

Enough commiserating! It was time to get to work.

*****

The morning had dawned cold with a light tinge of frost on the grass. Fall was fast descending upon Bryant Hills. Minnie was clearing away the breakfast dishes. She now made it a habit to make sure Ginnie had a good breakfast before going off to her job at the newspaper every morning. The friendship she had with her sister-in-law for so many years was steadfast; Ginnie stood by her while she went through all the difficulties two months ago following George's death. The least Minnie could do was to support Ginnie by making a good breakfast for her as she went on her way to work every day.

This morning, however, as Minnie was clearing the table, she noticed two vehicles parked in the driveway. She recognized one of them as Blake Harrison's Jeep Compass; the other was unfamiliar to her. She watched as Blake got out of his car and a tall, very distinguished-looking man in an expensive-looking suit and coat did so from the other vehicle. The men walked up the path to the back door and knocked. Opening the door, she greeted Blake, and he introduced the gentleman he was with. "Minnie, this is Rodney Grey Cloud. He is interested in the Mercedes." She shook hands with Grey Cloud and invited both men in.

"We've just finished breakfast," Minnie said. "Would you care for a cup of coffee?"

With that, the two men sat with Minnie at the breakfast table in her kitchen and discussed the Mercedes: what year it was, how many miles had it been driven, had any repairs been needed? Minnie gave Blake the keys to the vehicle to go for a test drive with Grey Cloud. When they returned and were again in the kitchen, Grey Cloud asked what the price was for the Mercedes. Minnie told him, and he countered with a price much higher than she had quoted.

"You are very kind," she said. "Why are you offering a higher price?"

Grey Cloud explained he had researched vehicles before answering the advertisement. This model of Mercedes was extremely well-built; he needed a vehicle that not only mirrored his image as a business owner but was also very dependable. He was not able to buy a new car every so often; he needed a vehicle to last. And this vehicle, he explained, was in excellent condition, almost as good as new. It was worth paying the extra money.

"What is your business?" asked Minnie.

Grey Cloud replied, "I am the CEO of the casino in Capitol City. Have you ever been there?"

"No," she answered.

Suspecting gambling was not a pastime this extremely genteel lady would indulge in, Grey Cloud explained gambling was just one part of the casino entertainment. There were shops, three restaurants, large reception rooms for weddings, concerts, and stage events, even an Olympic-sized swimming pool and hot tub for relaxing, along with a hotel for overnight guests. He invited Minnie to have dinner with him one evening in the French cuisine restaurant.

Minnie declined the invitation, for now, but perhaps in the future…

Before accepting the check from him, Minnie explained to Grey Cloud she was using the funds to pay the rest of the loan on the Mercedes. The auto loan corporation would send the title to the vehicle to her in about two to three weeks. Then she would sign the title over to him, and it was his. Grey Cloud understood what needed to be done. They would be in touch.

After Blake and Grey Cloud left her house, Minnie sat for a long time at the breakfast table, staring at the check Grey Cloud had given in payment for the Mercedes. Now she could pay off not only the loan on the Mercedes but the loan on her Buick as well. She did not have to sell her car! She could breathe easier with fewer monthly bills to face, especially going into wintertime. How generous Grey Cloud had been! But then, she reasoned, as the CEO of a casino, he more than likely could afford it. What a nice man he had been, she mused, and so pleasant to visit with. He obviously was well-educated and oh-so proud of his Native American heritage. She liked him. She was happy he had wanted to buy the car.

And once again, she thought, so helpful of Blake to post the advertisement.

CHAPTER 13

The check from Rodney Grey Cloud coupled with the reimbursement from the bank for George's illegal loan made it possible for Minnie to breathe easier, for now. She called the insurance agent George had used for their life insurance. Reviewing the requirements for a smaller policy than the original, she decided to take it, naming Ginnie as the beneficiary. Looking back at the events of the previous two months, Minnie felt Ginnie was a victim of her brother's selfishness as much as she; she hoped naming Ginnie as her beneficiary would provide a modicum of security to replace what George had always promised. Ginnie was so dear! A friend and sister-in-law—a powerful combination.

*****

Less than ten days after Minnie submitted a cashier's check for the remainder of the payment for the Mercedes to the auto loan company, along with a copy of George's death certificate, Minnie received the title for the vehicle in the mail. Marveling at the loan company's swift action, she called Rodney Grey Cloud at his office. He wasn't in, so she left a message to call her back.

Grey Cloud returned the call thirty minutes later. He agreed to be at Minnie's house the next day at nine in the morning. This time, when he arrived, unaccompanied by Blake Harrison, Minnie had the door open to receive him as he came up the walk. "Come in," she said. "Get in out of the cold." He entered the house, and she took his coat and hung it in the kitchen closet. "Please, sit down. I'll get you a cup of coffee."

Taking a place once again at her kitchen table, Minnie and Grey Cloud sat talking like old friends as Minnie signed the title to the Mercedes over to him, completing the transaction. And by the second cup of coffee, they were no longer *Mr.* Grey Cloud or *Mrs.* Gardiner; they were Rodney and Minnie. Rodney ventured a question, "Minnie, I have a confession. I did my research before I told Blake Harrison I wanted to see the Mercedes. When I asked who owned it, he told me your late husband, George Gardiner. I was surprised to hear he had died. You see, George was a guest at my casino quite regularly, in fact almost every weekend. I met him"—here his voice softened—"and I met a woman he introduced as his wife, but the woman I met was not you."

"Oh," Minnie replied, "that must have been Carole Cameron, his mistress."

Rodney remained quiet for a couple of minutes. "I realized as soon as I met you something was awry," he said, speaking in the same soft voice. Reaching across the table and putting his hand on hers, he said, "I'm so sorry you had to go through that."

Minnie told herself she was not going to cry. "It's over. It ended when George died. She has gone on her way to ruin the lives of other men. Thank you for being so kind, Rodney. I appreciate you being discreet."

And then Minnie found herself telling Rodney all about everything—how she had met George when she was eighteen years old and he was a senior in college, their married life together, growing older, growing apart except for social events, and finally George's death followed by the revelation of how he had squandered not just their insurance but their life savings, leaving her on the verge of bankruptcy. She told him how discovering her late husband had a mistress just added insult to injury. It all came out. Even how he had erroneously been allowed to take a loan against her house which he did not own. Lastly, she told Rodney of the resentment she felt toward her late husband and how she had no qualms to sell his car.

Minnie had not meant to cry, but she noticed when she stopped speaking her face was wet with tears. Rodney rose from his chair, opened a few drawers, and located a washcloth. He soaked the cloth in warm water; and giving it to Minnie, he said tenderly, "Here. Wash your face. You don't have to cry anymore. You're not the first woman whose husband cheated on her, and you won't be the last. You have your house. That's more than some people have, and your sister-in-law, Ginnie, your friend for so many years. You've said how you depend on her to help make financial decisions. And let's not forget your friend, Mr. Harrison. It's obvious he is trying to help whenever and wherever possible. From what I've seen, you are a very strong woman. You can get through this. I'll help you too."

When Minnie recovered, she was surprised to notice she didn't feel self-conscious about telling her troubles to Rodney. In fact, she felt much better after getting her feelings out in the air. And when Grey Cloud proposed they meet for dinner two nights later, she quickly agreed. After leaving her car with the valet, she was to go in the main entry of the casino; he would be there to meet her. They could have a leisurely dinner in the French cuisine restaurant located on the upper level of the casino.

Minnie was excited! She was going to a casino. She was going to have dinner with a very pleasant man. Oh, what fun.

CHAPTER 14

Blake Harrison had arranged for people from the investment company George represented to pack his personal files from the office into two large boxes and deliver them to Minnie's house. Minnie had the deliveryman unload the boxes in the sunroom where it would be easier to go through them. It was over a week since the boxes had been delivered, and Minnie was looking for something to do while Leona cleaned the rest of the house.

Reluctantly, she took the cover off the first box and began sorting the files into a stack of house bills and their many meaningless activities at the country club. It was amazing how they had squandered money over the years on frivolous activities they felt necessary to maintain their status in Bryant Hills society. If only they had cut back even a little, she would now have those funds with which to live. She continued sorting: office expenses, home, auto and life insurance policies, what should have been Ginnie's retirement fund proceeds, and…

"What was this?" The label on the file folder read "Loan for Taxes." She pulled the folder the rest of the way from the packing box and took it with her as she moved to the couch. Opening the file, she saw the original documents of the loan George had taken illegally using her home and property as collateral. The original amount of the loan was $250,000. The funds had been given to him the same day as the application and was put into a separate bank account. No wonder she had never known about this!

The pages following the application were copies of federal and state taxes for the years 2010 to 2015. The dates the tax forms were completed were all the same. June 2015. At the back of the file was a letter from the Internal Revenue Service, stating the business and personal taxes for George and Minerva Gardiner were now up to date. He would no longer have to face a court charge of tax evasion.

Minnie looked again at the bank book used to disperse the quarter of a million dollars. A check from George had been written for $250,000 to the Internal Revenue Service dated June 2015. Within the tiny record book was a Post-It note saying, "Pay this off before Minnie finds out." The second and subsequent checks were for the loan payment.

Oh, George. Oh, George, Minnie thought. *How you deceived me. Had you so little faith in me you could not tell me about this? And what else am I going to discover before this nightmare ends?*

She sat immobile on the couch for the rest of the afternoon. Later, when Ginnie came home from work, she found Minnie lying on the couch, sleeping. The tears on Minnie's face told Ginnie she had cried herself to sleep. Ginnie covered Minnie with an afghan and crept into the kitchen without waking her. Once there, Ginnie wondered to herself, *Good Lord, what more can happen! How much more can this woman bear?*

CHAPTER 15

The next day was Saturday. Minnie had awakened during the night and found her way to her bedroom without turning on any lights. Once there, she quickly changed into her nightgown and crawled into bed. She slept late on Saturday morning.

"Well, hello, Princess," Ginnie greeted her when Minnie emerged from her bedroom, still in her robe and slippers, trying to begin the day on a cheerful note. She poured Minnie a cup of coffee as she sat down at the kitchen table.

Minnie sipped the hot liquid, took another cup, but declined anything to eat. She was quiet for some time. Ginnie sensed there was something brewing inside her that she wanted to get out but decided to wait; if there was something Minnie wanted her to know about, she would tell her.

Slowly, Minnie began to speak. She told her lifelong friend about the boxes of files in the sunroom from George's office and how she began to sort them out the previous afternoon—piles for house bills, office expenses, insurance, country club expenses—and the file for the loan George had taken on her house. She asked Ginnie if George had ever mentioned having a problem with the taxes. No, Ginnie could not remember George ever saying anything about any kind of problem. She reminded Minnie how any, and all, mail was always sent to his office, even the utility bills for the house. George always handled everything. There would have been no way for either of the women to remember a letter arriving from the IRS or any similar organization. Not until after his death had the postal addresses been changed from his office to their home.

Minnie told Ginnie she discovered the reason for the $250,000 loan George had taken against her house five years ago. Ginnie was surprised to hear there were back taxes due on their personal and business incomes. From what Minnie had seen in the file, the reason they had gone unpaid was George didn't have the money to pay the taxes at the time they were due—so they had not been paid.

Why George never mentioned this to her at the time was still unbelievable—it would have been so easy to remedy. If she had only known, there would have been no problem allowing him to use her home for collateral. Why didn't he say something? Why did he assume he needed to keep this secret from her? Did he feel she would not understand? Was she so selfish a woman she concentrated only on herself leaving George to flounder through difficulties with no help?

At these last questions, Minnie once again began to cry. Had she really been so self-absorbed, doing only what amused her, her husband never thought to ask for her help when difficulties arose? My God—no wonder he turned to that trollop, Carole Cameron, so easily. No wonder he indulged her with everything she wanted. As long as he gave Carole what she wanted, she gave him what he wanted. And Minnie had not noticed when they began to grow farther apart than they were already.

It was her fault George had squandered every cent they owned. It was her fault he had lost almost everything. Everything was her fault!

Ginnie knelt next to Minnie's chair and cradled her friend and sister-in-law as best she could. She left her cry for a few minutes and then, taking a napkin, dried her tears and spoke to her sternly, "Okay, now that's enough crying. You were not in this marriage alone. You and George were in it together—equally—100 percent, each of you. Not 80/20, or 75/25, or even 50/50. Together, *both* of you. That's what marriage is, a union of two people, caring about and taking care of each other.

"It's not your fault he found a woman who wanted a sugar daddy to take care of her. It's not your fault he decided to blow every cent he ever earned on a woman he knew for only two or three years.

George was a grown man. At some point, he had to ask himself what he was doing. He *had* to know what he was doing was wrong. No matter how close a couple is or how far they grow apart, there is still an emotional connection. There had to be guilty feelings on his part. A person just cannot be married for over forty years and not feel guilty about cheating on their partner. I think that is why he had the heart attack. He could no longer handle the stress of cheating on you, coupled with the mess he made of your finances, and he was afraid to tell you what he had done. In the end, he was afraid of losing you. He really loved you. After all, Ms. Cameron did tell us she had left his business before he died. He was already trying to make right what he had done wrong."

Slowly Minnie stopped sobbing and listened to what Ginnie was saying. Oh, this woman! How, and when, had she become so intelligent? She always knew the right words to say to her to make her feel better.

Ginnie poured another cup of coffee for each of them and offered to help Minnie go through the rest of the files in the boxes. "Deal!" Minnie answered. "Then this task will be over and done."

Back in the sunroom, the two women made short work of sorting the remaining files. Minnie gave the file "Loan for Taxes" to Ginnie to look through. When finished, Ginnie suggested it might be a good idea for Minnie to show this file to Blake Harrison. Minnie agreed.

Toward the bottom of the last box lay a final folder labelled "Lease—CC Apt." Ginnie took the folder out of the box, absent-mindedly reading the label aloud. "Oh," she said. It was as though Ginnie immediately knew what the folder held. She thought she had spoken quietly enough so Minnie had not heard, but it was not so. Minnie asked, "What is that?"

Ginnie handed her the folder. Opening it, Minnie saw a copy of the lease agreement for an apartment located in one of the best neighborhoods of the city, the Bryant Hills Arms. After reading the papers, she realized George had not only hired Ms. Cameron to be his secretary, but he also paid her rent. It had been one of those company benefits a single woman like Ms. Cameron would not easily turn down. And since the apartment was in George's name, he had paid the $1,500 rent each month.

This time, Minnie was not breaking out in tears. "Fifteen hundred dollars," she said. "Fifteen hundred dollars. Fifteen hundred dollars." Ginnie thought Minnie was beginning to get a little fuzzy. Perhaps all of this was just too much for her.

Then Minnie rose from her seat and dashed to her desk in her bedroom. She opened the top drawer and withdrew her checkbook and then opened the file drawer, fingered through the folders, and withdrew an official-looking paper. Paging through the checkbook as she walked back to the sunroom, she told Ginnie how that number, $1,500, sounded familiar to her.

"A-hah!" she exclaimed. "Right here. You see, Gin, when I balanced my checkbook last week, I had a $1,500 discrepancy. I looked and looked but was unable to find anything to clear it away. Now here on the bank statement is listed 'BHA payment.' Bryant Hills Arms."

Ginnie compared the statement with the lease agreement for the apartment. "Minnie," she said, "you're still paying for that apartment. If I'm right, we have discovered a way for you to have additional income each month."

CHAPTER 16

"This is another item for Blake to look into," said Minnie.

"Good idea," Ginnie agreed.

The women straightened the folders putting them into categories to be looked at individually at another time. As they worked, Minnie asked, "What time is it?"

"Almost four," replied Ginnie. "Why? Do you have a hot date?"

"Yes!" answered Minnie. "As a matter of fact, I do. A dinner date, in Capitol City. With a very handsome man." With that, she rushed out of the sunroom to dress for dinner with Rodney Grey Cloud.

*****

She dressed quickly and, thirty minutes later, was driving toward Capitol City and Grey Cloud's casino. It was an hour drive, and she mused to herself as she made her way along the highway. *What a day! What two days!* Yesterday afternoon, she had cried herself to sleep after finding the papers for the bank loan to cover their back taxes. This morning, she had sobbed her heart out to Ginnie, who was ever so kind even when she spoke to Minnie sternly about her relationship with her late husband, Ginnie's brother. And now she was on the road, driving to another city, to a casino(!) to have dinner with an extremely distinguished gentleman she met little than a month ago.

Is this what they call progress? she asked herself. If so, she was driving toward it with her eyes wide open. Ginnie was right, it was time to stop crying and time to begin living once again. Whatever

George had done, whatever had happened between them, it was over. It could not be redone. Time to get on with her life.

When Minnie arrived at the casino, she left her Buick with the valet attendant and walked through the main entry doors. Rodney was waiting for her as he said he would be. She welcomed his embrace, saying hello to him as if they had known each other their entire lives. He took her by her hand, and they walked through the gaming area to a bank of elevators. They rode the elevator to the third floor and exited into a lovely foyer decorated with comfortable chairs, a couch, exquisite paintings, and live plants. Down the hall, they walked to a large door which Rodney opened with a key. This was his apartment, he said, his home away from home when he was at work. They were going to have dinner here instead of the French restaurant so they could talk privately. He pushed the door open, and Minnie followed him in.

CHAPTER 17

The apartment was so lovely Minnie caught her breath. Decorated in shades of soft gray and muted gold, the spacious sitting room had a gas fireplace at the far end surrounded by a huge couch, a comfortable-looking sofa chair, a beautiful wooden antique rocker, and a low table. A minibar was built into the wall on the left side of the fireplace with a floor-to-ceiling bookcase on the right. At the other side of the room, an oak desk filled the corner holding a computer, a printer, and a lamp with a shade depicting Native American scenes. An office chair completed the work area. The third wall of the apartment held two large folding doors next to a small table covered with a white cloth and set with exquisite china, crystal, and silverware for an elegant evening dinner.

The scene looked as though it could have been straight out of *To Catch a Thief*, where Cary Grant wooed Grace Kelly with the fireworks reflecting off the Riviera and the Mediterranean Sea in the background. It was beautiful.

Grey Cloud took Minnie's coat and handbag and spirited them out of sight. He went over to the desk and pushed a button on the phone pad. Then, offering her a glass of wine, he invited her to sit by the fire. The button on the phone pad reverberated in the casino kitchen two floors below, and their dinner was on its way. He had it all planned out; it was going to be a perfect evening with a lovely lady.

And perfect is what it was—perfect dinner, perfect wine, perfect setting, and talking by the fireplace… A man and woman getting to know each other. Just perfect!

They talked over dinner, and they talked sitting by the fireplace. They talked and talked. Minnie told Rodney about growing up in Bryant Hills, and Rodney told Minnie of his life as a young Sioux lad growing up on the reservation. He told stories of his parents and grandparents, along with his many relatives, and how they fished, farmed, and used the gifts nature provided to sustain their lives—such as gathering and drying wild rice from the lakes and tapping and cooking syrup drained from the many maple trees surrounding their village.

As he spoke, Minnie watched his expressive face, his high brows and cheekbones, his wide jaw. She admired his audacity to wear his hair in the traditional braid down his back, defying modern hairstyles for men. Rock stars didn't have a thing to brag about. They were so fake. Rodney was real! He lived and loved his Native American Sioux heritage.

She thought he was magnificent!

Throughout the evening, the wine turned to coffee, and the two talked until it was past midnight. Minnie felt herself getting drowsy and said she should be on her way, she had over an hour's drive before she could reach home. But Rodney insisted she stay—it was too late for her to be driving on the highway and, because she was so tired, it was too dangerous. Minnie was unable to protest when he suggested she take the bed in the bedroom and he would sleep on the couch. There was more than enough room in the apartment for two people to share.

The whole thing was quite innocent. And so Minnie went to sleep on Rodney Grey Cloud's bed the first night she had dinner with him. But she locked the bedroom door behind her because, after all, even though Rodney was so very much a gentleman, he was also a man.

CHAPTER 18

Minnie was awakened the next morning by the sound of a door closing. As she rubbed the sleep from her eyes, she slowly brought her surroundings into focus. This was not her bedroom. Oh yes, she realized as she became more awake, she had spent the night in Rodney's apartment at the casino. She rose and walked barefoot to the adjoining bathroom suite. She undid her bra and slipped out of her panties and then showered and dried herself with a luxurious, plush towel. This "casino stuff" was the pinnacle of luxury, she thought. Sure beats regular life.

After putting on the same clothing she had worn the night before, she found a comb in the vanity drawer and made herself presentable. Her lipstick was in her bag. As she opened the doors of the bedroom, she noticed they were no longer locked. In the great room of the apartment, she smelled coffee. She could use a cup, or two or three. Rodney was at his desk keying furiously, obviously busy. He was dressed in gray slacks with a softer gray pullover sweater that coordinated nicely with his gray hair. Even though Minnie had hung her clothing over a chair in the bedroom before slipping into bed last night, she felt unkempt next to him.

"Good morning," she said, "may I have a cup of coffee? It smells wonderful."

"Please," Rodney replied, "make yourself comfortable. My house is your house. I'll just be another minute, and then we can have breakfast. I've been catching up on a little work while waiting for you to get up."

At the little table where the evening before had been a fine meal with beautiful china now sat a decorative coffee pot, a pitcher of orange juice, and two servings of fresh-baked cinnamon rolls. *It just keeps getting better*, Minnie thought. *I must be in a dream.* While they savored the cinnamon rolls, Minnie mentioned she remembered locking the bedroom door before she went to sleep last night. Rodney looked straight into her face and said, "Yes. I needed to come in to use the bathroom."

"But the door was locked, I'm certain," she answered.

"Yes, it was. I unlocked it."

"Do you have keys for everything?"

"I do. It's my casino, my apartment," he said in a soft voice. "I'm responsible for everything that happens here. I need to be able to gain access to any part of this property when necessary, and," he added with a slight smile, "I needed to use the bathroom."

He was being practical.

"I noticed you had kicked off the blankets, so I put them over you again." He was quiet for a few seconds. "You look quite lovely when you're sleeping."

Minnie blushed.

Inwardly, Rodney smiled to himself. It had been some time since he had seen a woman blush. This lovely, fine woman had blushed because of something he had said—it felt good to know he could still cause that kind of reaction.

When Minnie regained her composure, it was time for her to begin the drive home and asked Rodney to please find her coat and handbag. Rodney refused to budge from the table until she agreed to meet him again. Yes, she would, he should call her so they could make new plans. As they walked to the elevator, he made sure she had the ticket from valet parking to redeem her car and remained with her until the vehicle was delivered to them at the main entry of the casino. He opened the door of her car and helped her in and then, taking her hand in his, kissed it as though he was an aristocratic French prince and sent her on her way.

CHAPTER 19

Monday morning, Minnie was sitting in Blake Harrison's office. She had brought the two folders and put them on his desk while telling him how they had been discovered as she sorted through the boxes of items delivered from George's office. Blake took the first folder and paged through it. He calmly said he would make some calls to confirm the tax payment George had made five years ago to clear himself and Minnie of any obligation to the IRS. Even though George had been sent an official letter saying everything had been cleared up, Blake wanted a personal confirmation for himself and for Minnie so she would no longer have to worry about it. Minnie thanked him, saying once again he was so very helpful and how she appreciated him standing by her through all the twists and turns she was experiencing at this time in her life.

Blake turned his attention to the other file, the one holding the lease agreement for Carole Cameron's apartment. Minnie showed him where, on her bank statement, the amount corresponding to the monthly rent appeared and how it also held the same name appearing on the documents. Blake became quiet; but his manner spoke a thousand words as he inquisitively and intelligently turned the documents over and back again, searching for information, finding it, and continuing to search for more information. Finally, he spoke. "I think you're right, Minnie," he said. "I think this document could very well mean you own an apartment in the Bryant Hills Arms. I'm going to call the number listed at the bottom of this page and see what I can find out."

He dialed the number and waited for an answer. But the call went to voice mail; so he left his name, phone number, and the reason he was calling the management office representing Minnie. Putting down the phone, he rose to take the coffeepot from a corner of his desk and refilled his and Minnie's cup. They knew each other well enough to visit as friends until the call could be returned. If the call was not returned within a half hour, they would go on with their day, and he could let her know what had happened later.

He told her how he had visited relatives in the northeast part of the state over the weekend and had gone deer hunting. They had camped out in the woods, made supper and breakfast over a wood fire, and slept in tents. While hunting during the early morning hours, they sat in blinds made of corn stalks and similar material to get as close as possible to the deer. He had shot a buck with six points on its antlers. The deer meat was being processed by a local company, being made into sausage, roasts, and venison jerky. He was quite proud of himself as he told his adventures to Minnie. Then he asked what she had done over the weekend.

Minnie spoke without shame as she told Blake she had driven to Capitol City on Saturday evening, met Rodney Grey Cloud, and went to his private apartment within the casino complex to have dinner. She was proud of herself, too, but for different reasons. She had taken control of her own life, after living vicariously for and through George during the past forty years. She had done something entirely on her own, and she enjoyed it.

While she was telling Blake about her dinner with Grey Cloud, Minnie neglected to see Blake's expression becoming more and more dark. As she was telling him how tired she was at the end of the evening and how she agreed to spend the night…well, Blake exploded. "Bloody hell! What are you doing, woman, spending the night with a man you just met?"

Minnie sat quietly, not saying a word. She had never seen this side of Blake. She could not understand why he should be angry. They were friends, she, and Blake, not husband and wife, not even seeing one another. She was no longer married; as a widow, she was free to see whomever she wanted to see. She had accepted and wanted to have dinner with Rodney Grey Cloud. Why was Blake angry? She had done nothing to be ashamed of… She had spent the evening in the company of a nice man, in very pleasant surroundings, enjoying excellent food. What could possibly be wrong with that?

Blake was clearing his throat. "What I meant was…" Ahem, again. "What I'm trying to say is…"

Oh my, Minnie thought. *Could it be?*

Meanwhile, Blake's dark expression was quickly fading from embarrassment to mere dismay. He rose from his chair and went to stand by the window looking out of his office. When he turned to face Minnie again, he had regained his composure. When he walked back toward his desk, he didn't seat himself in his office chair; he rounded the desk and sat next to Minnie. Taking her hand in his, he said softly, "I'm so sorry for speaking so crudely. It was not my intention to startle you. It's just that, oh, Minnie, you are such a dear person. You are so kind. You always try so hard to make sure everyone in your company is comfortable. Every time you invited me to your home, I always had such a pleasant time. I… I, Oh, Minnie, over the last few months, I've learned what a wonderful woman you are, how strong you are. There's no other woman I know who could have weathered the pitfalls George made you go through after his death. Minnie, don't you see? I'm upset because it was another man you went to dinner with. I want it to be *me*!"

CHAPTER 20

"Blake," replied Minnie as gently as she could, "why did you not say anything? I would enjoy having dinner with you."

"I was giving you time," he answered. "Anyone, woman or man, who had lost their partner after forty-plus years of marriage needs time to recover. I didn't want to seem as though I was hitting on you."

The two sat in silence.

The shrill ring of the office telephone startled them from that silence as though they had been in a trance. Quickly, Blake recovered and reached across the desk with his long arms to answer the phone. It was the management firm of the Bryant Hills Arms, returning his call. He listened to the person on the end of the other line and then began speaking. "This is Blake Harrison. My client, Mrs. Minerva Gardiner, the widow of the late George Gardiner, the original applicant on the lease agreement for the rooms in the Bryant Hills Arms, would like to know if she can take over leasing the apartment, when the lease expires, if she can sublet the apartment until the lease expires, and what, if any additional documents would be required. If you need a copy or the original of Mr. Gardiner's death certificate, I can certainly provide that for you."

A series of "Yes," "Okay," "Yes," and another "Yes" answer by Blake followed by an "I'll get back to you in a few days," and he was finished speaking. Turning to Minnie, he explained an original copy of George's death certificate was needed for the management company's files. After that, it would be appreciated if they did sublet the apartment since Ms. Cameron had abruptly left four months ago and the rooms were now sitting vacant. A vacant apartment in a building such as the Arms did not look well. It was up to Mrs. Gardiner what was charged for the monthly rent, but the management company would continue to withdraw $1,500 per month from her checking account. The lease would end in February with a lease renewal letter being sent to Mrs. Gardiner in December.

Once again everything was going too fast. Minnie told Blake she needed time to think about this issue of subletting an apartment. She would need a couple of days to discuss it with Ginnie, who, as always, was her friend and confidante.

Blake asked if he could call her on Wednesday morning. She should compile any questions she or Ginnie had, and they could go over them on the phone. Since the current month's rent had already been withdrawn from Minnie's checking account, there was no great hurry; but he felt this issue should be dealt with as quickly as possible.

He held her hand as he walked her to the door of his office. Would she care to meet for a cup of coffee, at the local bakery one morning? There were so many things he wanted to tell her, about himself, about his relationship with George; he felt he had an obligation to let her know these things. He wanted to clear the air so they could begin anew.

Minnie accepted the invitation for coffee but was careful not to commit to any kind of relationship. After all, Blake had been right; she was a woman who had just ended a forty-plus-year marriage, and she needed time to recover from her husband's death. She needed time as well to learn how to take care of herself and manage her home and finances. And she was a woman who the previous weekend had spent the night with another man (even though they didn't sleep together), a man she liked and respected very much, a man who was also a gentleman. Oh, she and Ginnie would be talking into the night, this night!

CHAPTER 21

That evening, Minnie prepared a quick dinner for Ginnie and herself, and after the two women had cleared away the dishes, out came the bottle of wine. They settled in the living room after lighting the fireplace. The wine along with the smell of good cedar logs created an easy ambiance between them.

As Minnie spoke about the lease agreement for the Bryant Hills Arms and the information Blake Harrison had gleaned about it, Ginnie began to ask questions. Ginnie's concern about her dear friend had not wavered from the day George had died. She wanted to help Minnie decide what was the best path to take, what would be best for Minnie, what would Minnie be able to live with.

Ginnie produced a tablet, and the two women quickly filled it with questions about the lease agreement:

- Had a deposit been made on the apartment along with the original lease agreement?
- If so, in what amount?
- Had an additional month's rent also been required along with the deposit?
- If so, in what amount?
- Under what circumstances could either of those deposits be returned to Minnie?
- If Minnie decided not to extend the lease for another year, how much notice needed to be given to the management company?

- And if the lease was not extended, was there any amount of the original deposit that could be returned to Minnie?
- Who was liable for the advertising required to put another tenant into the apartment at this time? The management company or could it be handled by Mrs. Gardiner's lawyer?
- If Minnie decided to sublet the apartment, would Blake be willing to handle the transaction?

And finally, something the women had not considered until now:

What was Blake's fee for all the guidance he had given to the two women to this point? And what additional fee would be required for him to handle any further business?

They tried to think of as many situations or scenarios that could arise and what the circumstances could be. They tried to be as professional as possible.

After that, the serious wine drinking began. Ginnie told her BFF about a travel writer who had visited the newspaper a few days the previous week. His name was Alistair Peabody; yes, British, with the accent to prove it. She described the man to Minnie and then spoke admiringly of his work, his writing, his people skills, his desire to retire and live in a small town like Bryant Hills. Minnie asked why the writer wasn't seeking a small village in Great Britain to retire since he was a Brit? Ginnie answered she had asked the writer that same question, and his reply was he had travelled worldwide and spent many years in so many different lands, but he had never lived in the United States—he wanted to experience life in the US while he was still young enough to do it.

Minnie noticed how Ginnie spoke about Peabody. It was easy to see Ginnie liked him. She gently teased her sister-in-law, and the two women giggled about it like teenagers.

Close to midnight, Minnie told Ginnie how Blake had reacted to her spending Saturday night at Rodney Grey Cloud's apartment at the casino. Ginnie was not surprised to hear what Blake had to say and explained she had always felt Blake would be the perfect match for Minnie—if George had not met her first. Minnie was surprised at Ginnie's reaction. When the women finally turned out the lights, said good night to each other, and toddled to their respective bedrooms, Minnie was still thinking of Ginnie's response.

Minnie had never considered marrying anyone but George. She had been so young, only eighteen, just out of high school, when they met. Even though she had a plethora of boys to date while in school, the world *did* stop turning when she met George. He was everything she wanted in a man. She had jumped into marriage with her eyes wide open.

And their life had been fulfilling, even wonderful, right up to the day he died.

It was the days after he died that had been so difficult to live through. Learning he had lied about their finances. Learning, by accident, about his mistress. Discovering he had lied to his sister as well as his wife, leaving them both to cope with near bankruptcy.

Minnie grew angrier at George every time she thought what she and Ginnie went through the days immediately following his death. And the worst part was, she would never be able to tell him how she felt. She had not been the type of wife to complain or nag her husband. But now, after he had done these things to her sister-in-law and herself, she wanted to scream at him at the top of her voice. She wanted to tell him how he had hurt the two women in his life he should have held dear. He lied to them. He had betrayed them.

George had betrayed her so badly she had thought nothing of going out for dinner with a man she had just met only three short months after his death. And another man, whom she liked and respected as well, thought her actions crude.

If her womanly instincts were correct, Blake had tried to tell her that morning how he wanted to have more of a relationship with her than just being a helpful family lawyer and friend. What was she going to tell Blake? Or Rodney, for that matter, when he called her to meet again?

"Okay," she told herself, "you are this enlightened woman who is now on her own. You should be able to figure this out. You should be able to make an adult decision about this."

Before falling asleep, Minnie once again heard Blake saying how he was giving her time to absorb the events in her life before asking her out to dinner. That was the answer! She needed time to put everything in her life into perspective. She was not going to allow either man, or anyone for that fact, push her into making quick decisions. She was going to take the time to think for herself. After all, she had always done everything for everyone her entire adult life—cleaning and cooking in the Gardiner home while George and his mother and sister worked during the day and George finished college; caring for her home and property her father had bought; giving dinner parties; and planning and hosting social activities to further her husband's business. Now it was going to be time for Minnie. No lunching at the country club or going to the spa twice a week. No, nothing of the sort. Minnie was going to take time to get herself onto an even keel, find out how to take care of herself, learn how to depend on herself before she would once again depend on or trust anyone, other than Ginnie.

CHAPTER 22

Wednesday morning, Blake called Minnie at a few minutes past nine. As he keyed the information into his computer, she dictated the questions from the list she and Ginnie had assembled regarding the lease agreement on the apartment. He had a couple of calls to make but asked if she would be able to meet for coffee at ten at the local bakery. Minnie agreed.

Blake was sitting in a booth with a steaming cup of decaffeinated coffee, waiting for her along with a frosted bear claw. Minnie and Ginnie had not had much to eat the previous Tuesday recovering from their date with the wine bottle Monday night. She made short work of the pastry while Blake watched her with a smile on his face. He liked a woman who wasn't afraid to eat in front of a man. He could never understand women who ate before going out to eat or to an event where food would be served; what was the difference? A person still had to eat, didn't they?

After Minnie left his office Monday morning, he had been able to contact the Internal Revenue Service representative whom George had communicated with five years ago about the unpaid back taxes. The representative confirmed all late taxes and fines had been satisfied. Happily, Blake now told Minnie this was one issue she did not have to worry about.

He had also placed another call to the apartment management company and was once again waiting for them to return it. He thought the management company was somewhat disorganized at the speed with which they didn't return calls. He suspected their negligence at returning calls kept residents in their apartments through another pay period, thereby increasing the income for the owner of the building. Minnie kept this information in mind; it could be an important item to remember when making her final decision whether to keep the apartment or to end the lease.

Sitting in the bakery, drinking coffee, and talking casually with Blake presented a different atmosphere from when Minnie was in his office—more friendly, without the pressure, nice. Minnie took the opportunity to ask Blake about his fee as the lawyer helping her wade through the events of the past four months. His personal guidance had been extremely helpful to her. She knew he was someone she could depend upon.

Blake rose from his seat and took his cup and hers. He went to the ever-present coffeepot at the far wall of the bakery and refilled their cups and then came back to the table. He had done this purposely so he could think how to answer Minnie's question. This would have to be a very diplomatic answer.

Sitting at the table once again, he began to speak softly while looking directly at Minnie. "Over the years, when George had questions or needed my guidance, I was reimbursed on an 'as needed' basis. But now, Minnie, counseling you is a service I rarely give to my clients. I must explain. Most of my clients are men. They don't need an explanation of the legal arrangements they have made. But you, your situation was completely different from those clients. You had left your business affairs to George. He had taken care of everything.

"Please, Minnie, believe me when I say I only discovered how George had destroyed his business accounts and your insurance policies within the hour of our meeting the morning after George died. I knew nothing of what he had done. I have to say, it piqued me to know the insurance agent had also no knowledge of what he had done. In my mind, an insurance agent needs to pay attention to his accounts as closely as an accountant. Certainly, the insurance agent received monthly reports about the activity of the policies he wrote. Even if George dealt directly with the insurance company's home office to draw money from the policies, the insurance agent would have had this information in his monthly report. And yet he said nothing. Yes, George had initiated the policies, but you were his beneficiary. You should have been consulted when he made the withdrawals. I can only assume George signed your name as you, for you. And I can also assume the same thing happened when he changed the beneficiary for the retirement account from his sister, Ginnie, to his secretary.

"I felt so bad for you and Ginnie. My heart went out to both of you. I felt as though I had let you down. I should have been more aware of what George was doing. No, Minnie, there is no fee for any of our consultations. I am obligated to help you through this as well as I can. I owe it to you and Ginnie."

"Wow." Minnie spoke as softly as Blake. "That's quite a speech. Thank you so much. I appreciate you telling me this. I have wondered several times if someone, anyone, might have said something to George as he was raiding the insurance policies about what he was doing. I'm sure, Blake, it would have been you, had you known."

"I'm so glad you met me for coffee today, Minnie," was his reply. "I've worried about what I could say to you. We have been friends for so long. I've been a guest in your home. I certainly did not want you to think I purposely left this happen. It feels so good to be able to discuss this in a casual setting instead of my stuffy office."

With that, Minnie laughed softly, and the two parted as friends. Blake would contact Minnie when he had the answers to her questions about the lease agreement.

CHAPTER 23

Minnie left the bakery parking lot and took a right turn with her car. The bakery was on a one-way street in the business district, and she needed to drive around the block to get back into the traffic pattern. She braked for the upcoming stoplight as it turned yellow. She could tell from the speed of the vehicle in front of her that it was not going to stop; it was going to continue through the light. At that moment, she observed from the corner of her eye a street person pushing a huge grocery cart filled with what was obviously her personal belongings, stepping out into the crosswalk.

Minnie braked hard and screeched to a stop. But the vehicle in front of her continued on its path through the intersection. She left out a scream. Good Lord, had the woman been hit by the vehicle in front of her? The woman was no longer visible; had she been hit, and was lying on the street? Quickly putting the car into the park position, Minnie jumped out and rushed to the side of the street woman to see what she could do to help.

The driver of the vehicle in front of her had also stopped, but the car was now blocking the intersection. Somehow, miraculously, a cruiser with two local policemen was behind her and had witnessed the accident. One of the patrolmen immediately took charge and stopped traffic in all directions. The other came to the side of the woman who had fallen when the vehicle going through the intersection had creased the side of her shopping cart. The woman was crying, sitting in the street. Her cart had been knocked over, and some of her belongings were strewn in the street. She was obviously distraught. She didn't have much, but what she did have was now blowing away!

As Minnie and the police officer helped the woman to her feet, people from other vehicles who had also stopped began gathering her items, righted her damaged cart, and helped put her things back together.

The first officer spoke with the driver of the vehicle who had hit the woman's cart. It was clear he was going to be ticketed for going through a red light. The second officer asked if the woman needed medical attention. No, only her pride had been hurt; please don't call an ambulance. She could not afford another medical bill was her reply.

Minnie still had her arms about the woman. It didn't occur to her the woman's coat was shabby and dirty. Her hair was matted down, and from the odor Minnie breathed, it was obvious the woman could use a shower. Regardless, Minnie continued to hold her. She was shaking uncontrollably. Minnie was asked if she knew the woman. No, she didn't but had witnessed the accident and had just stopped to help.

Due to the woman's condition, the officer once again asked if an ambulance should be called. And once again, the woman insisted no. Minnie heard herself telling the officer the woman could come home with her. Minnie would take care of her. Minnie had plenty of room. The woman could stay for a couple of days or as long as needed to recuperate from the shock of what had happened. Once the woman had calmed down, the officer could come to Minnie's home and ask his questions.

Could you believe it? The officer agreed!

The policemen had the driver's information from those who had been involved in and witnessed the accident. They had Minnie's home address and cell number. They would call at Minnie's home the following morning to give the woman time to collect herself and regain her composure.

One of the policemen helped the woman into Minnie's car. Her belongings were put into the trunk, and the dented shopping cart would be discarded.

And that was how Minnie met Donna Harper.

CHAPTER 24

Parking her Buick in the garage, Minnie walked around to the passenger side of the vehicle, opened the door, and helped the distraught woman out of the car. Once inside the kitchen, Minnie quickly put the kettle to boil for tea. This woman needed something warm inside her tummy—it would help to calm her. She helped the woman remove her coat and sit down at the kitchen table.

"My name is Minerva Gardiner, Minnie to all my friends," she gently said to the woman. "I have a feeling you could use a friend."

Another gush of tears poured from the woman. She struggled to get through them and finally spoke. "Yes. Everything in my life has been so dreary the last couple of years. I cannot help myself from crying. It is the only thing I can do. Please, my name is Donna Harper. I was a teacher at the Bryant Hills High School June of 2018. How I ended up living in the street is a long, dismal story, but there it is. You've been so kind. Thank you so much for helping me. I don't know what I'm going to do. I have nowhere to go." Donna continued crying helplessly while she spoke. It was obvious she was still in shock from the accident.

Minnie gave Donna several tissues and held her hand until the tea kettle blew its whistle. A cup of strong tea would work well. She filled the tea ball with a generous helping of Earl Grey, put it into the teapot, drew two cups from the cupboard, and set them on the table. While the tea steeped, Minnie took a block of cheddar from the refrigerator and sliced it onto a plate. She set some crackers and a few grapes next to the cheese and put it on the table by the cups. "Now," she said gently, "you just tell me all about it. I won't be shocked at anything you tell me. Believe me, I've heard it all."

Thirty minutes later, Minnie and Donna Harper were talking as though they had known each other for years. Hmm, Minnie mused, Ginnie, Blake, Rodney Grey Cloud, now Donna Harper—sitting and talking with them at her kitchen table was therapeutic. Something good happens here!

Donna's story was the same as other people who needed to adjust their living style after losing their mate. Donna had taught keyboarding, office procedures, and Microsoft Office at the Bryant Hills High School for the past twenty-five years. Her husband drove an eighteen-wheeler delivering goods to all areas of the Upper Midwest—until he contracted lung cancer two years ago. He had passed away early in April 2018. The couple were childless. Donna finished the year teaching at the high school and took the summer off to recoup from losing her husband. There had been no time to grieve, to say goodbye. She had been allowed just three days off from the school for her husband's funeral but was required to be back in class on the fourth day or face being relieved of her job.

Meanwhile, Donna carried the same amount of bills to pay by herself as there had been when both she and her husband were employed. The rent was the first item to change. She struggled to downsize their belongings and moved to a tiny efficiency apartment during the summer from which she could walk to work. Except, her teaching contract was not renewed for the fall. The administration realized two younger, inexperienced teachers could be hired for the price of one, seasoned teacher, with money to spare. And since the school district needed to make budget cuts wherever possible, Donna was out of a job.

She piled her most-needed belongings into a cart she spirited from the grocery store and hit the streets. There was nothing else she could do; she had no income, no place to live, no one to help her. She could collect unemployment, but that was even less than her regular salary, and she hoarded every penny.

Life on the streets was degrading, demeaning, everything the word terrible could describe. At the time, the only good thing was the weather; at least she wouldn't freeze to death sleeping out in the elements. She took a daily meal from the mission at the Catholic Church downtown and some nights was lucky to have a cot in their dormitory. Then she could use the gymnasium locker area to shower and wash her hair.

In November, when the weather turned cold, she began to search for a better way to live. She applied for several teaching positions as a substitute teacher but was unable to correspond with the employment agencies because her phone plan expired along with internet access; without a permanent address, she had to let go of the idea. Aside from no longer being a competitive candidate, she had no professional-looking clothing to wear to an interview. It was over a year since she had taught—there were more desirable applicants than her.

Donna hardened herself to living on the street. She made a few friends along the way but for the most part trusted no one. She knew where to find food and lodging in bad weather, and she had become adept at judging human nature. She survived, but she was unhappy with herself and her life.

Last night, she had slept at the mission dormitory, had breakfast, and was walking with her belongings, trying to sort her options to survive another winter. At the intersection, she was thinking and talking to herself as she walked and did not see the vehicle try to run the red light. The driver of the vehicle had expected her to stop. She didn't stop and had walked right into the car.

"What a story," exclaimed Minnie as Donna completed the tale. "You have obviously been through a living hell. Well, don't you fret, I'm here now to help." When Donna had her fill of tea, crackers, and fruit, Minnie bundled her upstairs to the bedroom opposite from Ginnie's. She went into the bath and began to draw water into the tub. Placing towels, soap, and shampoo where Donna could reach them, she told Donna to make herself at home. As she left the bathroom, she said she would return with sleepwear and clothing. Donna should call if there was something she needed.

Donna felt as though she had died and gone to heaven! This kind woman—this lovely house the woman was so eager to share.

What had she done to deserve this treatment? An angel from up above surely must be looking down on her. She deftly undressed and slid into the bathtub. Oh, Lord! It had been a long time since she had been able to relax like this.

That evening, Donna met Minnie's sister-in-law and best friend, Ginnie. Donna felt as though she was the luckiest woman in the world. She went to bed that night marveling how she had made not one but two new friends.

CHAPTER 25

The two policemen were welcomed into Minnie's kitchen the following morning and were surprised at the change in the woman who had been struck by a car the previous morning. Obviously, spending the night in Minnie Gardiner's house agreed with her. Their questions were short, to the point and polite: what was her name, her occupation, her address? At Minnie's suggestion, Donna gave her address as that of Minnie's. The officers were assured Donna Harper would be living at Minnie's house from now on.

In the days following Donna coming to live at Minnie's house, Donna did everything she could think of to make herself useful. She took turns tidying the kitchen after meals, helped with the bi-weekly cleaning and laundry, and showed Minnie how to manage an Excel program on her computer to calculate and keep the monthly budget. Although she was no longer living on the streets, Donna loved being outdoors. She walked among the apple and plum trees in the backyard, picking the remainder of the fruit that was still edible and had not yet fallen from the trees. She made jam from the plums and jelly and applesauce from the apples. There was so much jam and applesauce Donna put it into pint jars for preserves.

Even though Minnie insisted Donna did not owe her anything, Donna refused to take no for an answer and gave part of her meager unemployment earnings to Minnie once a month. It was, as Donna said, the least she could do for Minnie since she felt Minnie had literally saved her life. Within a few weeks, Donna again applied for substitute teaching positions and was hired at the junior high starting

January 1. Donna was ecstatic; these two lovely women had helped get her life on track! How could she ever repay them?

As far as Minnie was concerned, there was no need for repayment. Helping Donna recover from living in the streets had been a very fulfilling act for Minnie. Ginnie felt the same. Many times, during evenings, as Ginnie worked on an article for the newspaper, Donna had provided invaluable information about the computer Word system as well as how to find obscure facts through Google. It was obvious Donna had a good head on her shoulders and knew how to use it. As the women began to know each other better, Minnie and Ginnie grew to enjoy not just Donna's knowledge but her offbeat sense of humor. As far as Minnie and Ginnie were concerned, Donna Harper was here to stay.

CHAPTER 26

Blake had finally gotten a response from the management company for the apartment George had rented. He and Minnie discussed the lease agreement over coffee, once again at the local bakery.

Blake was well organized and had brought the notes taken during his conversation with the apartment manager. Yes, the apartment could be sublet. Advertising to sublet the apartment had to be specific and could be done by either Minerva Gardiner or Blake Harrison as her representative. Any amount of rent could be charged for the apartment, but a consistent charge of $1,500 monthly would continue to be deducted from Mrs. Gardiner's bank account. If Minerva Gardiner intended to sign another year's lease, the management company needed to be notified as soon as possible. Also, if Minerva Gardiner did not intend to renew the lease, it would be appreciated if the management company be notified immediately. As it was their goal to have residents in each of their apartments, the manager would have to begin advertising now for February tenants. And finally, if Minerva Gardiner chose not to renew the lease, three months' rent needed to be paid at the time of notification. Yes, there was an account holding the original deposit and additional month's rent; this would be refunded to Mrs. Gardiner after the proper documents were signed. If Mrs. Gardiner decided not to renew the lease agreement, it would be her responsibility to have the apartment thoroughly cleaned and in presentable shape before the deposit and additional month's rent could be refunded.

Minnie had spent some time debating with herself the pros and cons of subletting an apartment. She now used Blake as a sounding board. It could be a source of income for her, but would the profit justify the amount of rent payable to the management company each month? In her mind, charging $300 more each month than what she paid to the management company was not a sufficient profit. A possible renter could easily have the same apartment for $1,500 by renting direct from the management company. Was it worth the effort?

Another thought: Minnie had recently invited Donna Harper to share her home. Donna currently received unemployment and had been hired as a substitute teacher in the local school district beginning with the new year. It would be just as easy to collect $300 from Ms. Harper as it would be to gain $300 from renting the apartment. Looking at the situation this way, it was six of one and a half dozen of another. Donna was already living in her home; she or Blake would have to advertise for renters for the apartment to become profitable. The only difference was Minnie would not have to pay out $1,500 to receive $300.

There was one more item Minnie had discussed with Ginnie she told Blake. Could she tolerate maintaining the relationship with the management company for an apartment her late husband had shared with his mistress? Would she be able to stand the thought of what George had done behind her back every time she received the rental payment from the new residents? Would this just be a continuation of blaming herself for what had happened between herself and her late husband? She had the funds; would it be easier on herself if she just paid the manager the $4,500 necessary to break the lease agreement and let it go at that? After all, she would recover one month's rent plus the $500 deposit. Was it better for her psychologically and emotionally to spend $4,500 to recover $2,000?

Listening to Minnie discuss the pros and cons of the situation, Blake could not help thinking, *This woman understands the situation. She's got a hold on it.* Two weeks remained before another rental payment was due. Blake suggested he notify the management company they would be at the office the following Monday morning. That would give her the weekend to come to a decision. Minnie liked the idea, so that is what they did.

CHAPTER 27

Minnie was proud of herself. Following the meeting with Blake Friday morning and using him to help brainstorm what to do with the lease agreement for the apartment had been so helpful she had the decision made by Friday night. She slept well that night; she was learning to think for herself, and she felt the decision was good. Saturday morning, she called Blake at his private number and told him she had decided not to renew the lease agreement. Even if Donna Harper decided to live somewhere other than Minnie's house when she was once again teaching, Minnie would find some other way to make up the money. After all, eliminating the apartment rent from her budget would also eliminate having to make the $1,500 payment. It was a win-win situation. She thanked Blake for being so patient with her that morning by listening to the issues she had expressed. Blake said he found it interesting to hear her point of view and then asked her about a matter he had forgotten to talk about on Friday.

He had forgotten to mention the annual Holiday VFW dinner and dance at the local hall downtown. It was tonight, and he had two tickets. Would Minnie care to go with him?

For the last ten years, Minnie and George had always attended the event. This year, the party had slipped through her mind. Well, she had more important issues with which to deal. Yes, Minnie replied, she would love to go. Fantastic, Blake answered, he would pick her up at five that afternoon.

Blake hung up his phone, stood tall, crooked his arm, made his hand into a fist, and drew it to him with a resounding "Yes!" The lady was okay with going to dinner and a dance with him; and Blake, well, he was just fine with the lady.

*****

An hour after talking with Blake that Saturday morning, Minnie received a call from Rodney Grey Cloud. Would she care to have dinner with him tonight in his apartment at the casino?

Minnie had to decline, saying she had a previous engagement. "With whom," responded Rodney in a surly tone of voice, "that lawyer fellow, Harrison?" Minnie did not feel she owed Grey Cloud an explanation of who she was having dinner or where she was going. "I have an engagement with a friend," she said. One more time, Rodney asked, "Is it Blake Harrison?" And again, Minnie did not feel she needed to explain who she was seeing that night. "Who I spend my time with is of no matter. I have many friends. As it so happens, I have plans for this evening," she said strongly into the phone.

It was obvious Grey Cloud was offended by what she said. "Well, if you don't want to see me anymore, just say it," he barked into the phone. Minnie told herself to remain calm; this sounded as though it could become a full-blown argument if she let it. Calmly, she answered, "I never said that, Rodney. I suggest you call in a few days, and we can put something together." Silence at the other end of the line and then "Okay." And the line was clear.

Throughout the rest of the morning and early afternoon, Minnie felt uneasy about Rodney's reaction when she had to decline his invitation. Donna was busying herself in the kitchen, chopping vegetables for the evening meal with Ginnie. Yes, Minnie thought, she would see what Donna had to say about it. After all, she had been married too.

Donna kept a straight face as Minnie recalled her and Rodney's conversation from the morning. When Minnie finished talking, Donna very gently said to Minnie, "He's jealous. And not just of Blake but of any man you spend time with."

"But," countered Minnie, "we've only seen each other one time. There's nothing for him to be jealous about."

"Doesn't matter," answered Donna. "Sometimes, it only takes one date for a man to feel he owns a woman."

"But I don't want to be owned, not by anyone," Minnie protested. "I've just been widowed from my husband after forty-plus years of marriage. It was not a dreadful marriage, but after discovering what he did without my knowledge, I don't want to be in that situation any time soon. I want to have some time to be me. Is that too much to ask?"

No, Donna answered her, and then went on: men don't think of things from the same perspective as women. Most men in Minnie's generation were raised to view women as possessions. Men look at their wife, their family, their home as a status symbol to be reckoned with against what other men have. She asked Minnie if she had ever heard the adage "The difference between men and boys is the price of their toys"? It means, Donna explained, men judge each other by what they have—women, houses, cars, etc.

"Do all men think like this?" asked Minnie. The answer was no—only the men who feel the need to flaunt their possessions, to show other men how successful they are. Some men never think like this. Some men are so secure in their manhood; they don't have to be jealous of others.

Donna continued, "My husband used to say, if I'm doing what I should be doing to make my wife happy in our marriage, I have nothing to be jealous about. But when a man is not doing what he *should* be doing in his marriage, then he only has himself to blame if he gets jealous."

Gently, Minnie asked, "Did your husband ever get jealous?"

"No," was the quiet answer. With that, Minnie went to dress for the evening.

CHAPTER 28

Ginnie came in the back door of the kitchen from a rare Saturday working at the newspaper. "Whew!" she exclaimed, "the Sunday edition has finally been put to bed. Mmm, dinner smells wonderful. What are we having Donna?" The younger woman lifted the cover of a kettle simmering on the stove and let Ginnie take a sniff. "Hamburger soup with minidumplings and banana bread on the side," answered Donna with a smile. "Something to warm our bones."

"I swear I'm going to have Jim hire you to write a cooking column for my women's pages. You have so many hearty recipes. Have you always cooked like this?" Ginnie asked.

Nodding, Donna replied, "I was the oldest in my family, and when both Mom and Dad worked late, it was up to me to make supper for the rest of the kids. When Mom was at home, she and I would cook together, so I learned most of it from her. But I did a lot of experimenting on my own." She ladled the soup into two huge bowls. "Come now, you've had a long hard day. Tell me all about it."

Ginnie told how she was only supposed to work until noon, but then about eleven this morning, the proofreader began to feel dizzy. Turns out the proofreader was coming down with the flu, so she was sent home so as not to spread it to everyone else in the office. There was nothing Ginnie could do; she had been promoted to editor of the women's pages from the position of proofreader. Since she was already there, she took over the job.

After the page setups were completed on the computer and forwarded to the printer, Jim Hall, the editor, had come into her office smiling like a child at Christmas. Alistair Peabody, the famous travel writer who had visited the newspaper and the town several weeks earlier, was back in the office. (Now Ginnie was talking with a glow of her own.) "Alistair, I mean Mr. Peabody, was looking for an all-American town to live in for a few years before returning to Great Britain. He had traveled all around the world and wanted to experience life in the United States," said Ginnie. "Well, long story short, he has chosen Bryant Hills. He stopped by the newspaper office to give us the good news."

It was easy for Donna to see Ginnie was quite pleased with the news she was sharing. Looking at Ginnie, she saw what everyone else saw—a beautiful woman, sixty-two years old, intelligent, interesting, and interested in others. Someone like this Alistair Peabody would be a kindred spirit; they would share many areas of interest. Donna was happy for her. She thought it would be nice if, after Mr. Peabody was settled, he and Ginnie could be good friends.

Ginnie changed the subject. She asked Donna how long she had been a widow. Donna answered it was three and a half years since her husband died of cancer. And, yes, every day that went by, she would remember something about him—his smile, his gray-green eyes, his laugh, especially his laugh when he was telling something humorous he had heard on the road or when he was teasing her. They had been married for twenty-four years, just kids really, fresh out of college. They had set up housekeeping on a shoestring, but that didn't matter. They had each other…

Donna was very quiet for a few moments, and Ginnie asked no more questions. But then Donna began talking again. She told how she had finished her teaching degree at the university in Capitol City and was hired by the local school district right after graduation to teach at the high school. That was when she and her husband had met. He was an over-the-road trucker, and she taught classes at the local high school. They had a good life, simple, as long as they weren't extravagant. Everything ended when he was diagnosed with lung cancer.

After supper, the two women cleared away the dishes and then set the Scrabble board on the floor in front of the fireplace in the living room. Nobody really knew who won, because they spent the time telling stories, talking about their lives, their families, and their work. It was a nice evening at home.

CHAPTER 29

Blake and Minnie were in the office of the apartment management company at ten Monday morning with the original lease document folder in Blake's briefcase. The meeting was short and sweet. Minnie handed the manager George's death certificate and showed her identification as his widow. Blake confirmed she was the widow of George Gardiner. Minnie signed the papers to end the lease agreement, gave the manager a check for $4,500, received a check for $2,000; and the pair was on their way.

Blake had driven the two of them to the meeting. Now Minnie asked him to stop at the bank so she could deposit the check from the management company. He did so and then suggested lunch at the hotel buffet before he went back to his office. Minnie declined; she had things to do at home she hadn't been able to get done over the weekend.

They drove in easy silence. Blake didn't get upset at Minnie's refusal to go to lunch with him the way Rodney Grey Cloud had reacted the Saturday before. Their evening out for dinner and dancing at the VFW was still in Minnie's mind. What a pleasant evening it had been. Good food, a good band with a good beat, good friends she had not seen for several months—and a very pleasant man to share the evening. Minnie had attended events before when she had danced with Blake, but this time was different. She noticed, as a woman, how attractive he was—was he always this tall(?), how he held her as they danced, and how nice it felt when he held her. She also noticed several of the other single women watching her with jealousy in their eyes.

Blake had been a perfect gentlemen the entire evening, even when, at the end of the night, he had walked her to her door and they were standing in the cold while she thanked him for a lovely time. Even when, with his arm still about her waist, he leaned down and kissed her softly and then said just as softly, "Yes, it certainly has been a very lovely evening." Opening the door for her but not stepping inside, he reminded her of their appointment Monday morning and said he would be by to collect her at nine thirty.

Blake was always a perfect gentlemen, Minnie thought as they drove—helping her in and out of the car, making sure everything at the management company was done correctly and legally, always making sure she was comfortable in her surroundings. Not a hint of "male games" anywhere. Yeah, a welcome relief after the battle on Saturday morning with Rodney.

Wait a minute, Minnie thought. *Give Rodney a chance. Don't discount him, because of that little blowup last Saturday. You told him to call to make plans for another date. Wait and see what happens. If he can rationally explain his behavior last Saturday, that will make a difference. He may have had something happen during his workday to become upset. There are two very handsome, very pleasant men in your life. You do not have to choose one of them to spend the rest of your life with. Right now, they are both just friends.* She reminded herself she was going to continue doing what she had said she would do—she was going to take care of herself. And in the meantime, if either Blake or Rodney asked her out, whether she went or not was going to depend on what she wanted to do.

*****

Donna had made waffles and sausages for breakfast for the three women that morning, so Minnie was not hungry for lunch when she returned home. Donna had a message for her: Sergeant Howell from the local police station had stopped by the house about a half hour after Minnie left with Blake. He asked Minnie to give him a call upon her return.

Minnie asked if it concerned Donna's accident, but Donna said she didn't think so. Wondering what it could be, Minnie dialed the number. The phone rang four times at the police station before Howell picked up; he sounded as though he was running a race as he said in a quick, clipped manner, "Yeah?" Minnie introduced herself and said she was responding to the message he had left at her home earlier that morning.

The sergeant explained he had a dilemma; he had no room in his jail! This confession prompted Minnie to giggle, but she managed to stifle it before it came out. Why was this a dilemma, and how did it concern her, she asked? Seems as though the jail was full, was his reply. There had been a robbery at the bank over the weekend, and the perps had been arrested, but they were four men, and he had each of them in a cell. There was no room for any new prisoners. Late last night, one of his officers had arrested a street person on a drunk and disorderly charge. The fellow had slept off his inebriation in one of the cells overnight, but the other prisoner was so violent the sergeant feared the man could be injured if kept in the same cell any longer. He only needed to be under surveillance until his court date at the end of the week.

Since Minnie had been so kind to a street woman who near-missed being hurt in a collision with a vehicle a few weeks ago and offered her a chance to rest and recuperate in Minnie's spacious home—well, he thought perhaps she might have room for a fellow needing a kind hand. It was said as a question, but Minnie heard the plea for help in the officer's voice.

Her first concern was Ginnie, Donna, and herself as the only other people in the house. They were all women. Was the man violent? Was that a reason for concern? Was he still drunk? Who was he, and where did he come from? These and many more questions she put to the sergeant. After her questions were answered, Sergeant Howell asked again if she had room for another person.

Well, yes, Minnie told him, there was room for another person, but she wanted to meet this man before letting him into her home. The sergeant's response was he would send the man to her house in a squad car with two of his officers that afternoon. He suggested if there were any house rules to be enforced while the man was under her roof, he be advised as quickly as possible.

Minnie and Donna prepared themselves to meet a jailbird!

CHAPTER 30

Frank Jones struggled to stay calm. When was that officer coming back? How long had he been gone? How long had he been in this stinking cell? And who was this gorilla in here with him? What kind of animal was he? Lord, it had been a long night. His cellmate had paced the entire night, banged on the bars, and looked at him as though he was lunch. Twice, Frank was seconds away from calling the night watchman to save him from being sexually violated. It would be worth giving up drinking if he could get out of this cell.

He could really use a drink right now. Oh, he could taste a nice cold beer going down his throat. But he knew he couldn't have just one beer; he needed all the beer in the barrel to make himself feel better this morning. And then where would it come from after that? Sadly, he thought how he always had to be on the lookout for the next drink.

He noticed sunlight beaming in through the twelve-foot-high glass block windows. Maybe, now that it was daytime, the officer would return and let him out of this cell. Then he could be on his way…

When the officer returned and mercifully unlocked the cell to let Jones out, it wasn't to let him go on his way. He was still being detained, it was explained, just not here in the jail. A court appearance could not be arranged until Thursday. Until then, Jones was going to get "special treatment"—and he better appreciate it!

Within minutes, Jones was pushed into the backseat of a squad car, two officers jumped into the front seat, and they were driving away from the jail. Where were they going, Jones asked the officers more than once? No reply. Whoa, he thought, what had he done last night? He remembered the drinks and the bar—but nothing else. He had blacked out before, but this time could be the worst. Jones decided to sit back, keep quiet, and watch where they were going.

The cruiser parked in the driveway of a beautiful Tudor-style home. Jones, still in handcuffs, was helped out of the vehicle and walked to the back door by the two officers. Donna led them into the kitchen. Introductions were made. Minnie and Donna sternly appraised this intruder. The officers informed the women they would return Thursday morning to pick up the prisoner for his court appearance. Either they or Sergeant Howell could be reached at this special phone number if an immediate response was needed. Mr. Jones was to abide by the rules of the house until then. If that could not happen, Mr. Jones would immediately be taken back to the police station and could share a cell with another prisoner. (*No*, thought Jones, *that will not happen.* An angel had smiled on him today, and he had been given a reprieve. He would sober up and serve the three days until his court appearance.)

Did the women have anything to say to Mr. Jones before the officers went back to the station?

Yes, answered Minnie. She faced Jones and looked squarely into his eyes. *He's not so tough*, she thought. *A few stern words and he won't be any trouble at all. The man is older, past retirement age. Maybe he just needs a chance to get back on his feet. He has lived on the street for so long he has lost faith in mankind. We can help.*

To Jones, she spoke sternly. "Mr. Jones, my sister-in-law, our friend Donna and myself enjoy an occasional glass of wine. However, if I but once smell alcohol on your breath or on your person or in your room, you will be out on the street immediately. Do I make myself clear?"

The man's response, with the two officers looking over his shoulder, was a repentant "Yes, ma'am." *No matter what it takes*, he told himself, *I must lick this demon and make it through the next few days. This time, I* must *recover. I've hit bottom. There is nowhere to go but up.*

CHAPTER 31

And so another person was shown to an upstairs bedroom (across the hall from Ginnie and Donna's rooms); given orders to bathe themselves; and once more, for the sake of the women in the house, cautioned as to what would happen to him if he decided to imbibe. Minnie went searching in George's closet for a couple pair of jeans, work shirts, and underclothes to make the man presentable. He might have to roll up the pantlegs, but at least they were clean. His other clothing would be tossed into the trash; it was nothing but threads, certainly not warm enough for this weather. Donna stood outside the door to the man's bedroom with a rolling pin in her grasp, ready to squash an attack on either of the women's honor. It was clear who owned the house, but Donna would defend it if she must.

As soon as Minnie had time, she phoned Blake and told him what she had done—taken a drunk prisoner into her house and was holding him until the officers could take him to his court appearance in three days.

Blake was immediately on the defense. He could not believe the sergeant had left no one to guard the prisoner. He volunteered to spend the next few days at Minnie's house, guarding, watching, and otherwise supervising the man. He would sleep on the couch, overnight if necessary, in order to hear anything out of the ordinary. Clearly, he was ready to defend the house and the women if it became necessary. To Minnie, he was like a knight in shining armor; to Donna, he was a godsend.

Before Blake could arrive at Minnie's house after a day at the office, Donna took charge of the prisoner. He was commissioned chores designed to stretch his muscles and broaden his mind. Wood for the fireplace was first on the list, and he made several trips from the house to the storage shed at the back of the yard and back to the house before Donna was satisfied. Then the fireplace needed to be cleaned out before it could be lit again. After that, the sidewalks had to be swept since woodchips and wood dust had accumulated on them from the work. By the time the sun went down, it was dinner time, and Frank was longingly thinking about sleeping on the comfortable bed in his room. He had done well today, and he was proud of himself. One day down, two to go.

The first thing Blake had done after hearing Minnie had taken a prisoner into her home was to call the local police station. Sergeant Howell told him the cells were filled with the men who had attempted to rob the bank Saturday night. There was no room for anyone else. The bank robbers were such violent men Howell didn't want Frank Jones to stay in the cell with them any longer than needed. Yes, Jones had been picked up for drunk and disorderly, but that usually happened to Jones two or three times a year. He was an alcoholic but not a violent man. Due to the arrests, Howell had no extra officers he could assign to guard Jones at Minerva Gardiner's house. Jones had been put on his strictest behavior and was expected back for his court appearance Thursday morning.

Blake told Howell he was going to personally look out for the women in Mrs. Gardiner's house to ensure they would be safe while Jones was in their care.

By the time he arrived at Minnie's house that evening, dinner for five was set on the dining room table, and Frank Jones was sober and as clean as a shiny new penny. When everyone was seated and grace had been said, Blake asked the man what he had done during the afternoon to occupy his time. Jones told the lawyer about carrying wood, cleaning the fireplace, and sweeping the walks. "If it would be up to the warden here," said Frank, motioning toward Donna, "a man would never be able to rest in this house." Blake had to squelch a chuckle as he looked at Donna; she sat at the table with a stern but satisfied gaze.

That evening, Blake did as he said he would—he slept on the living room couch so he would be able to hear if Jones wandered around or out of the house. Liquor wasn't kept out in the open, but there had to be a bottle or two of wine stored somewhere. Blake had promised the sergeant Frank Jones would appear sober at his court hearing. He meant to keep his word. Perhaps, since Jones was not a criminal or violent, he wasn't a very fearsome individual—but Blake relished the thought of being able to keep the women safe, especially Minnie. He wanted to do whatever he could to let her know he wanted to take care of her.

In the morning, Blake woke with a start and, hearing voices in the kitchen, arose with a jolt. He went upstairs to use the bathroom in Frank's bedroom and to tidy up before joining the others in the kitchen for coffee. Ginnie had already gone off to work, Minnie was sipping coffee at the table, and Donna was asking him how many eggs he wanted and how he liked them made. Wait a minute! He stopped still. Where was Frank Jones, he asked the women? Was he still sleeping? Minnie gave a knowing smile. Donna stood in the center of the kitchen, calm but silent. "Ask the warden," said Minnie, at which the two women broke into laughter.

"Look outside," said Donna. "I've got him working already."

Blake drew aside the curtain on the back door and saw Jones shoveling snow. It had snowed during the night! Jones had to shovel the driveway and sidewalks before he could have breakfast. He had shoveled a path for Ginnie to walk to the garage and back her car out to the street before she left for work. After being granted a cup of coffee to warm up, he was now finishing the remaining walks and drive.

"Well, it looks like you've got everything under control," he said to the two women. "What do you need me for?"

"For the night shift," Donna answered. "We have to get our beauty sleep."

Jones left a gush of cold air into the house when he came back in, but he sat down with a contented look on his face. He had slept well, the best he had slept in quite a while, as a matter of fact. He had gone one full day without having anything to drink, and he was beginning to feel good about himself. He had already decided if the judge hearing his case on Thursday included a thirty-day stay at a clinic for alcoholics, this time he would go without protesting. The gorilla in the jail cell had scared him worse than he realized; he never wanted to be that drunk again.

Blake went home after breakfast, dressed for his office, and went to work; but he would return that evening, just in case. Frank relaxed with another cup of coffee until Leona arrived—today, his job was to assist her with the heavy cleaning, lifting, and moving furniture. The cleaning would take all day because now there were two additional bedrooms to care for. When Leona arrived and she and Frank set to their task, Minnie and Donna compiled a list of groceries. What Frank needed was good, hot, healthy, homemade meals, Donna remarked. To heal his body and mind. And work to keep him busy. Minnie agreed and left to do the marketing.

CHAPTER 32

Rodney Grey Cloud had come to an understanding with himself. He needed to slow down! Working six days a week, twelve-hour days, was hard on men half his age. What was he doing, trying to work himself into a stroke, or worse? The cashier had just reported how they had mistakenly counted out a thousand dollars for one of the casino's prominent gaming guests, and they thought that was when they could have lost the three hundred-dollar bills. The cashier had complained the week before how difficult it was to sort the new hundred-dollar bills when they came direct from the bank. They stuck together. Rodney heard his voice begin to raise as he reminded the cashier that was why the vials of salve were sitting on the shelf of each cashier cage—to be used! Rodney had been shouting by the time he told the cashier this had happened too many times on his watch and the cashier was fired. By the time Rodney had left the gaming floor and returned to his apartment, he was fuming. He should have calmed down before he phoned Minnie that Saturday morning. He should have given himself time to regain some substance of normalcy. But he had not, and when Minnie said she already had plans for the evening, his temper went off the charts.

She was angry with him for being angry with her; he knew it. It didn't take much to understand the situation. But then he had forced her to be stern with him, and he had to back out of the phone conversation like a coward. Gad! How he hated doing that. Would she be able to understand why he had become so angry? He knew she had a multitude of friends. The social life she led as George Gardiner's wife for over forty years presented lots of opportunities to meet people. She had not specifically said she was seeing Harrison that evening, but he could tell she was going somewhere special. Oh, how he wished *he* would be taking her there.

She had closed their conversation by saying he should phone, and they could make plans. Well, at least she had not hung up on him. That must mean she was not ready to show him the door just yet, didn't it? Right now, he needed food, something cold to drink, and rest. He was getting too old for this work thing. Maybe it was time to turn the casino over to a younger group of men with new ideas. He had lost his first woman due to his arrogance. He would hate to lose another, Minnie, over it as well. He needed time to think.

He worked on the computer until midnight, eating a sandwich and drinking iced water as he labored. Hydration—he always felt better when he drank iced water.

Now it was Wednesday morning, and Grey Cloud had worked ten days straight because two of the managers were down with the flu. He would have time to call Minnie this afternoon and make plans to meet her tonight or Thursday. He would drive to Bryant Hills and pick her up instead of expecting her to drive for an hour to the casino to see him; that would make the engagement more intimate.

Wednesday afternoon when he rang Minnie, she answered immediately and cheerfully said hello. Conversationally, he asked what she was doing. Her response was peeling potatoes, carrots, and onions for the evening meal. She had a few minutes to talk.

He commented it sounded as though it was too late to ask her to dinner that evening. Yes, she said, but even if he had called earlier, she would not be able to meet him that night; she had to guard a prisoner!

What was this about? What was she doing now, playing sheriff?

Minnie told him about taking Frank Jones into her house to guard until his hearing Thursday morning. Frank was an amiable fellow but had been charged with drunk and disorderly behavior for the third time this year. The local police station had no room for someone like Frank because they had cracked a burglary ring last Saturday night and all the perpetrators were in their jail cells. This left no room for Frank Jones. She was doing a favor for the sergeant and needed to stay home and guard her prisoner until Thursday morning when two officers would arrive to take him to his court appearance.

What an explanation! What else was she planning, Grey Cloud asked, starting a home for disappointed suitors? Minnie laughed easily at the intended joke. Well, she countered, she did have plenty of room.

They talked a few minutes longer and agreed to get together Thursday evening for dinner. Rodney would pick her up at seven.

"There!" Minnie said out loud when the call ended. "Let's see what the man has to say for himself."

CHAPTER 33

On Thursday morning, two police officers arrived at Minnie's home promptly at 8:00 a.m. to collect Frank Jones for his 9:00 a.m. court appearance. Before leaving, Frank thanked the three women profusely for helping him stay sober until his court hearing, for the clothes and accommodations, for the tasty meals he so enjoyed, and for their faith he could recover from his alcoholism. As he walked out to the cruiser, Frank gave an "I'll be back!" imitation, making everyone smile.

Ginnie followed on her way to work; Donna sat down at the computer to do some research; and that left Minnie alone, to finish sorting through the box of file folders from George's office. Before tackling the stack marked "House Bills," she thumbed through the remaining folders, making sure there would be no more surprises like the unpaid taxes and the apartment. She could not take another jolt like those. Her curiosity satisfied, she scrupulously went through each of the house folders while making a list of what had been paid and what remained to be paid. She congratulated herself for being able to pare down the expenses by eliminating the country club, spa and salon, George's tailor, and a few other insignificant merchants she would no longer need in her life. There was money to be saved, and she would find it!

By the end of the day, she had all the house bills on a list for Donna to put into the computer budget. It would send automatic reminders when a statement should be received, paid, or need to be looked at. For now, she chose to receive the statements in the mail opposed to paying them online. Paying them online would allow her to forget about a specific bill and lose track of her bank balance; she didn't want that to happen.

In the middle of the day, both Minnie and Donna noticed how quiet the house was with Frank Jones gone.

Skipping dinner in lieu of her engagement with Rodney Grey Cloud, Minnie allowed more than an hour to dress for the date. It had been some time since she had a chance to soak in the bathtub. She added a few perfumed bath balls and slid into the steamy water. Oh, how relaxing, if only she could stay here all evening; but, no, at some time, she would have to get out of the tub, dress, and go out into the cold.

She wanted to give Rodney a chance to explain his actions of the previous Saturday. She wanted to hear what he had to say. Later, when Rodney called for her promptly at 7:00 p.m., Minnie felt a gush of excitement. "Hang on there, girl," she told herself. "You are not eighteen anymore."

They went to one of the quieter restaurants in the city. Known for good food and soft ambiance, it was the perfect place to dine and have an intimate conversation at the same time. Rodney waited until they had finished eating before he started to explain his actions a week earlier. He told her about the missing money from the cashier, how the cashier had been warned several times previously, and how he himself was personally responsible for the cashier's actions. He had allowed the cashier's lack of work ethic to send him into an outburst, and it had carried over to their phone call.

He took Minnie's hand and apologized profusely. Minnie had heard something else in his voice as he talked. She asked Rodney how long he had been CEO of the casino. More than thirty years, was his reply. From its start in the early 1990s. He had accepted the position because he was one of only a few people in his tribe who had a college degree. It was a mark of pride to be able to take the position. As he became adept at the work, he was asked to join the council governing the tribe's activities. He was well respected and listened to when he gave his opinions.

But the recent incident with the cashier had prompted him to consider stepping down; there were younger members of the tribe who were now able to take his place. They had new, modern ideas how the casino should operate and to use its profits to create industrial possibilities for his people to support themselves. As the retired CEO of the casino, he could retain his place on the council and work with his people to help them socially as well as financially.

Rodney and Minnie's conversation went on for two hours and many cups of coffee. Again, as they had that first evening in his apartment, the couple had spent the night talking. And tonight, after listening to the man spill out his dreams for himself and his people, Minnie could tell Rodney was tired. When they returned to Minnie's house, she did not invite him in for a final cup of coffee, and he was not offended.

This time, instead of kissing her hand, he took her into his arms, kissed her softly on her lips, held her as he said good night, and kissed her again before leaving.

CHAPTER 34

Thanksgiving had arrived!

Donna had contacted her two brothers and two sisters in the adjoining states. Relieved to hear from her and to know she was no longer living on the streets, her youngest sister had invited Donna to spend a few days with her family over the holiday. Minnie and Ginnie had bundled her onto the bus for the six-hour drive the day before Thanksgiving; she would return on Monday.

Phone invitations went to Alistair Peabody, Jim Hall, Blake, and Rodney. Being mindful of the young married couple living next door to them, Minnie and Ginnie included them as well. They were expecting—soon. They had moved to Bryant Hills just two weeks ago and had no time to get settled to have a holiday celebration.

When Minnie invited Rodney, he declined. No, he said. He was working that day, all day. Besides, Thanksgiving was not a holiday for his people. Before Minnie could think, she asked what if we were married? Would I have to give up Thanksgiving because I would then technically be part of your people? Rodney didn't skip a beat; his quick reply was, "Minerva Gardiner, if that is a proposal, I accept."

It caught Minnie totally off guard and left her speechless. A long silence fell over the phone until Rodney said he would call her the following Friday morning; they could meet for lunch. Ending the call, Minnie was thankful they had not spoken over speaker phone. She was so warm in her face from blushing she rushed to wash her face with cold water. This was the second time he had made her blush!

Thanksgiving Day dawned with a light dusting of snow covering the grass which now was turning a dreadful brown. The snowfall gave out a cheerful air, and everyone attending dinner at the huge, old Tudor was infected with it. The couple from next door were the first to arrive, toting two bottles of a smooth-tasting burgundy wine. Jim Hall, with his wife and Alistair Peabody in tow, was next, with Blake the last to arrive, carrying yummy pumpkin and apple pies.

The group ate turkey and dressing, drank wine, relaxed by the fire in the living room, had coffee and dessert, and finally left to go home about eight in the evening. Everyone had a great time, even Alistair, who admitted the holiday was not celebrated in his country. But this wasn't Great Britain, Ginnie had countered. When in America, do as the Americans do. Alistair heartily agreed.

*****

Friday morning following Thanksgiving, Rodney called Minnie at nine o'clock. He would be able to swing by and pick her up in a half hour; they could spend the day together. When she was in his Mercedes, he began driving back toward Capitol City. Minnie asked where they were going? "I'm taking you home," he said. "Home to where I really live."

They drove about a half hour from the outskirts of Bryant Hills when he turned off the road onto a less-used drive leading back toward the hills. Minnie remained quiet as she watched where Rodney was driving. This was Indian land he told her as he drove. Had been for thousands of years. It was part of the original treaties made in the early 1800s. Because it was more remote than any of their other property, it had become obscure, as though forgotten. Now only he and a few of his relatives lived in the area. In a short while, they came to what appeared to be a small ranch. Sheep grazed on a sloping hillside, horses were in the corral by a barn, and tucked among a stand of evergreens was a handsome log cabin. Beyond the barn and at an angle was a small but crystal clear lake with a wooden dock running out into the water.

Rodney stopped the car, got out, and walked around to help Minnie. She looked around with amazement. "Beautiful," she said breathlessly, "just beautiful."

"I'm so glad you like it," responded Rodney. "This is my home. Let me show you inside."

A huge entryway led to an even larger great room. One step down held a wooden table made from one cut of oak, over six feet long and almost five feet wide. The table had been polished to a high sheen. Eight matching oak chairs with upholstered seats sat around the table; the two at each end were captain's chairs. Opposite the table on the left side of the room was a comfortable sofa chair next to a table and lamp, inviting anyone to cuddle up and read a good book. The far wall held two bookshelves meeting each other at the corner; the rest of the wall was covered with a stone Inglenook fireplace. Large man-sized sofa chairs and couch surrounded the fireplace. Between the reading snug and the bookcases, two over-sized French doors opened upon a rock patio. Looking back from the fireplace, Minnie spied a loft tucked above the entryway.

To the right of the entryway was the guest room. Behind the fireplace was the master bedroom, which included a bath area and a spa set into a greenhouse. To the far left of the entryway was the galley kitchen and breakfast nook. The inside logs had been sanded and stained to a high luster just like the table. Rodney watched Minnie as she walked through the home. He had taken great pains to make sure everything would meet her approval. A place for everything and everything in its place he had said when he gave the cleaners their instructions.

"Do you like my lodge?" Rodney asked after giving Minnie the grand tour.

"It's beautiful. Have you always lived here?" asked Minnie.

"Yes, I was born here."

He invited her to sit on the huge burlap-colored leather couch and told how his great-grandfather had built the original cabin. His grandfather had added a wooden floor. His father updated it with plumbing and electricity. And he had remodeled the lodge, adding the kitchen and master bedroom area while carefully making sure the original log cabin stayed intact. The structure had been handed down to him as the oldest son; however, he was an only son, so he would have inherited it regardless.

"And the barn and livestock? Who looks after things here when you are at work for days on end?"

"My uncle and his sons. We own the land together."

"Are your cousins the younger men you referred to who would like to take over the casino operation?"

"Just one of them. He's a good man. He just needs a little seasoning."

"And, I suppose, when you started out, you didn't need any 'seasoning'?"

He looked at her with a facetious grin on his face. "No. I never needed anything like that."

For lunch, Rodney took slices of ham and cheese from the refrigerator and made them into sandwiches. Potato salad with bacon and onion dressing was heated in the microwave; there was coleslaw from late cabbage on the side. They ate in the breakfast nook and drank mugs of steaming hot chocolate following their meal. After they cleared away the dishes and put the leftover food into the refrigerator, he asked if she would like to walk around the grounds and see the lake. He told her the sheep had been an addition during his father's time. The spring and fall lambs were sold to the local meat market. The flock was sheared in spring and fall and the lengths of wool sold to a mill on the farther side of Capitol City. In wintertime, the manure and straw from their pens in the barn were dried and bagged into mulch for gardening. It was an enterprise making the sheep a profitable investment year-round.

The dock stretched two hundred feet out onto the lake, and its thirty square foot area was big enough to fish from. There were sitting benches to accommodate either fishermen or someone who just wanted to sit and quietly watch the water. Minnie thought it a beautiful place to enjoy an early morning cup of coffee in serene quiet, especially in early spring or fall.

The lake was so small it had no name and did not appear on any map. But it had been a protected area since the days of the first treaty and provided good walleye fishing for Rodney and his uncle's family. In wintertime, their smoked northern pike was an appetizing specialty to enjoy.

Returning to the lodge, Rodney laid a fire in the grate of the fireplace and lit it. The flames were soon snapping and crackling, sending warm drafts of air into the great room. They sat and talked in front of the fire on the big couch, sipping wine, until they realized the sun had gone down. "I'd better get you home, or your sister-in-law will be sending the law out for you," Rodney commented with a chuckle.

"Yes," was Minnie's reply. "And you know how tight I'm in with the law."

CHAPTER 35

One week after Thanksgiving, the couple next door gave birth to a baby boy. After giving the young mother a few days to rest and the young father a few days to get used to his enlarged family, the three women phoned on a Saturday afternoon and said they would come to visit and were bringing coffee. "Don't fuss. We'll take care of everything."

They walked next door, Donna holding a covered cake carrier, Ginnie carrying a beautifully wrapped box, and Minnie holding the coffee carafe. It took at least thirty minutes for the women to take turns cooing over the baby and holding his warm little body. When he was finally put into his bassinette once again, Donna commented, "A baby born at Christmastime is a very special child."

They sat down to have coffee and cake with the doting couple. Ginnie presented the lovely box. "Oh my, oh heavens, these are beautiful," commented the young mother as she withdrew two crocheted baby blankets in soft shades of blue. One had a simple stitch with an occasional row of white and a darker blue. The other had been made in a filet-crochet pattern, with nine squares (three across and three up) of teddy bears peeking out from the design. When Ginnie mentioned the blankets were practical as well as beautiful, she told the young mother they could be washed and dried in the automatic machines. The couple could not believe Ginnie had made the blankets herself, by hand. The young father said the blankets were prettier than anything he had seen in the stores. "You should sell these online. They make a beautiful and practical gift for a new baby," he said as he sipped his coffee.

Later that day, after Minnie, Ginnie, and Donna had returned home, Donna noted Ginnie was extraordinarily quiet at the supper table. Roused from her thoughts, Ginnie reminded her two housemates what the young father had said about the crocheted blankets: "You should sell them online."

"Do either of you crochet?" she asked Donna and Minnie. No, responded Minnie; she did not. Donna said her mother had taught her to crochet as a young girl, but it had been many years since she had picked up a hook.

Excitedly, Ginnie outlined her thoughts. If an advertisement would be placed in the Bryant Hills, Capitol City and surrounding area newspapers, for baby blankets in blue, pink, and white shades, did either of the women think there would be a response? The answer was yes, especially right now, to be given as holiday gifts. How many did they think could be sold in a week? Approximately five to eight, give or take, was the next answer. Would Donna be willing to help crochet blankets if Ginnie gave her a few stitching pointers? Sure! Would Minnie be willing to learn to crochet if Ginnie taught her the basics? Yes!

It did not take long and the women were discussing the wording of the ad; how many blankets needed to be completed before the ad was placed; and if Donna could design an organizational program on the computer to keep track of expenses such as yarn, the price of the ad, delivery of blankets to purchasers. The oh-so many little details excited people enjoy discussing when one of their group has hit on a really good idea!

Within one day's time, the women were ready to start. Ginnie had opened an account at the bank from which to buy the advertisement, yarn, and mailing supplies. Donna had designed a spreadsheet on the computer and opened a PayPal account to receive online payments. Minnie and Donna had been given fresh and refresher courses in crochet.

Monday night, after Ginnie had come home from the newspaper, the women were ready to start working on the blankets. Such excitement you have not seen! They did not even stop for supper; they jumped immediately into working with the yarn, sitting close to one another so they could talk as they worked, in front of the big fireplace in the living room, making baby blankets to sell.

CHAPTER 36

Every ounce of the women's energy was put into crocheting baby blankets. The newspaper advertisements had been placed for the teddy bear design by Ginnie on Monday and would run for five days. During that time, the women planned to make at least three blankets in blue, pink, and white to satisfy customer choices. They all rose at 6:00 a.m., so they could work for an hour before breakfast and sending Ginnie off to work. Any household chores were breezed through as quickly as possible so Minnie and Donna would have more daytime to crochet. The women worked so hard at their task they eliminated lunch and cut the evening meal down to quick sandwiches or takeout so they would have more time to crochet.

Their first surprise came within two days, on Wednesday with five online orders. Donna left out a whoop from the computer that resounded through the house. Fortunately, because they had worked so diligently, they had enough blankets to fill the orders. Minnie and Donna assembled the mail packages, and Minnie drove them to the post office. At $35 per blanket, they had earned $175! Granted, they had to account for the cost of the yarn, advertising, and mailing paraphernalia; but even with that, in two days, they had earned enough money to buy groceries for two weeks.

That was a profit! That was something to get excited about! Good grief, Charlie Brown, they were in business.

CHAPTER 37

On the way to the post office to mail the baby blankets, Minnie decided afterward she would stop at Blake's office. She had a few questions about their enterprise; she lived in a residential area and wondered if there were any zoning regulations about operating a business from her home.

Pulling into the parking lot of the post office, she spied Blake walking out with his daily mail. She quickly parked the car and called to him. The friends greeted each other and exchanged the customary remarks about the weather—yes, it was cold enough. When Minnie told Blake she wanted to talk with him, he suggested they meet for a cup of coffee, again at the bakery; the atmosphere was more pleasant than his office. Blake would drive ahead and get them a table. Minnie said she would follow as soon as she had posted her packages.

At the bakery, Blake had a large cup of coffee waiting for her at a corner table, this time with a scrumptious-looking Danish. He had a huge Bavarian cream-filled donut with chocolate frosting. When Minnie arrived and commented on the pastries, Blake quipped coffee and sweets were necessary to get through the cold weather. The two sipped their coffee and ate in amiable silence.

Then Minnie explained what Ginnie, Donna, and she had been doing for the last week. She told Blake about the baby gift to their young neighbors and how selling handmade crocheted baby blankets online had its start. She told him Donna had built a spreadsheet on the computer to help them keep organized. What she wanted to know was, since where she lived was zoned residential, if they needed any kind of specific permit to operate a business or sell items from her home. And if a special permit was necessary, could Blake help them obtain it?

Blake had already taken a small notebook and pen from the inside breast pocket of his suit and was making notes. He had a few friends at city hall. He would make a couple of phone calls when he returned to his office. He should be able to have answers to her questions before the end of the day. He asked Minnie how payments were received for the items sold, were they keeping track of expenses, and if a dedicated bank account had been established, whose name was it in, or had they given the account a company name? He explained if a permit were needed, a company name might be needed as well.

Minnie smiled at him. *He is always all business. I can depend on him for anything*, she thought.

He walked her to her car and then returned to his office to begin work for the day. After opening the mail, he put the final touches on documents for a few of his clients, took a bathroom break, and put the notebook from his pocket on the desk.

He stared at the notes for some time. What in the world were those women up to now? What was Minnie up to now? First she stood up to a well-known banker and told him his records were wrong, there was no loan against her house. Then she took a street woman into her home to recover from a car accident because "it would be more comfortable than being in a hospital," followed by guarding a drunk until he can get to his court appearance.

What next?

When he had gone over ways to cut expenses for her to be able to live on her income, he never mentioned anything like this. How do these women think of these things? To just take a suggestion from a neighbor and turn it into something profitable. *Well*, he thought, *yes, that is how some businesses have their start.*

This woman, Minnie Gardiner, was so different from the description George had given of her when he and George started working together. Yes, the physical description was the same; but she was no way the woman who spent money like it was water, never bothering to find out from where it came.

Blake had known George underestimated his wife the first time he had been invited to their home for a dinner party. With only a little kitchen help, Minnie had planned the menu, done most of the cooking, and served the meal. As he remembered now, it had been an extremely tasty experience. He smiled as he also remembered how friendly she had been as he entered her home. Nothing like her stuffy husband. It was obvious part of the reason George Gardiner was so successful in his business was due to his personable wife.

To Blake, Minnie represented the perfect wife. His obsession with her had begun during that first dinner party. And he made sure he could be invited for subsequent dinner parties so he could see her again.

When Blake heard through the business grapevine that George was seeing a young woman, spending weekends with her at the casino in Capitol City, he reacted in disbelief. The first thing he wanted to do was find George and give him a black eye. The second was to call Minnie and tell her what her husband was doing behind her back. How dare George do that to this lovely woman?

He had imagined Minnie coming to him for consolation. He had imagined how it would feel to hold her close to him, kissing away her tears and waiting for her to calm down before she started divorce proceedings. If, at any time, Minnie would have given the slightest signal she was interested in him as a man to be more than just a friend, Blake would have jumped at the chance. But he had remained quiet, falling back on client confidentiality. He would wait and bide his time.

This woman who was supposed to know nothing about how to earn money was finding ways to cut corners and increase her household income no mere man would consider. What was that saying? Oh yes, "never underestimate the power of a woman."

Blake smiled to himself. He looked at the notes he had taken earlier that morning. What else could Minnie and her cohorts get themselves into to earn an extra dollar?

Blake picked up the notebook, put it back into his suit pocket, and continued his work for the day.

CHAPTER 38

The flurry of activity from the first five orders for baby blankets continued through the current week and the next. The women had to devote every second of available time to crocheting to get the orders made, packaged, and mailed in a timely fashion. Ginnie took her yarn and hook to work using her breaks and lunchtime to get in a few extra rows. Donna kept hers either on a counter in the kitchen or next to the computer. Minnie carried the "baby blanket in progress" in a sturdy tote bag so she had it handy to work on if she was in a doctor's office or somewhere shopping, waiting in the checkout line. Their projected thinking was the rush of orders would slow down after the holidays; hopefully then, the orders would level off and become somewhat predictable, at least to the point where they could determine how many orders to expect for a week or a month.

Nonetheless, the idea had become a lucrative venture for them. Even though the amount of extra income it brought into the house was not mind-bending, it was enough to cover some of the smaller bills, and that alone gave the women reason to celebrate. They were moving forward, not backward.

*****

Christmas was right around the corner. Two of Sergeant Howell's police officers who happened to be at the right place, at the right time, had volunteered to tote home the tree Minnie had purchased from the Christmas Tree Lot, carry it into her house, and set it up in the front foyer. They were the two officers who had so helpfully assisted Donna on the day of the car accident. When the officers arrived at Minnie's house, they could not escape the unmistakable aroma of cookies baking. Their helpfulness was rewarded with steaming cups of hot chocolate (topped with marshmallows) and sugar cookies fresh from the oven.

When the officers went on their way, the women dragged the boxes of holiday decorations from the storage area beneath the stairway and sorted the strings of lights, balls, and bulbs to put on the tree. As they opened each box of decorations, their excitement for the holiday rose another level. They felt like kids in a candy store! They worked steadily, and within a short time, the tree looked as if it was fit to be photographed for a designer's magazine. It was gorgeous!

They celebrated by having cookies and cocoa, sitting on the carpet in the foyer, admiring their handiwork.

"How blessed we are," commented Ginnie. "We have so many friends, nice neighbors with a beautiful baby boy, a warm place to live, and each other to depend on as we make our way through life." Donna and Minnie agreed. For a while, this year, it seemed their world was going to crash down around them; but after the last few months, they could see they were going to be all right. They had so many things to be thankful for. The year would end on a good note for them, and the new year—well, they were working tirelessly to ensure their success. There was light at the end of the tunnel.

On Christmas Day, the ladies slept late, had coffee and cinnamon rolls for breakfast, and opened their inexpensive gifts to each other. No big spendy extravaganza for them, not this year. They were secure in the knowledge they had many good friends and their lives would improve in the new year.

That evening, while Minnie was preparing to go to bed, it occurred to her Blake had never called her back about her questions of operating a business in a residentially zoned area. It had been over two weeks since she had talked to him.

No matter, she would call him Monday morning after the holiday. He must have been so busy he forgot to call.

*****

Christmas Eve had been a Wednesday and Christmas Day a Thursday. Guessing professional offices such as Blake's law office would be closed for the entire weekend, Minnie waited until the following Monday morning to contact him. Blake answered the phone on the third ring. He did not sound well. He apologized profusely to Minnie, saying he had been down with a cold and sore throat for the last week and had not felt up to coming to the office or doing any kind of work. He was in the office this morning to collect a few of his files and try to work from home. When Minnie reminded him about checking the zoning regulations regarding their online venture selling baby blankets from home, he said he could not get through to his friends at city hall today—the offices were closed until after the New Year holiday.

He put a note on his calendar to contact his friends at city hall about the matter the first day in January when he would be back in the office. Minnie had to be satisfied with that. After exchanging Christmas and New Year wishes, they hung up.

*****

Rodney Grey Cloud felt like kicking himself. He should have seen this coming. Why had he not thought about this? He was scheduled to work the week of Christmas Eve and Christmas Day and the New Year week. There was no way he could change the schedule, even if he was the CEO. Because he had no wife or children, he had always volunteered to work these last two weeks of the year to accommodate other employees who wanted to spend time with their families. It was assumed he would be available for those hours and was automatically put onto the schedule.

Now, however, he had Minerva Gardiner in his life. This would be their first Christmas, and he sorely wanted to spend the time with her, not at work. He was desperate to find some way to make it up to her. He needed to come up with something special.

Ahh! He would reserve a suite of rooms for Minnie, her sister-in-law, and her friend Donna to stay the weekend at the casino hotel. Dinner at the French restaurant and a continental breakfast the following morning would be on him. The ladies would also have a pass to the spa and pool. And for Minnie, well, he still had to think of an extraordinary gift for her. But he had a little time. He would call and invite them for this weekend.

The three women shrieked with excitement when Minnie hung up the phone and said they had been invited to spend the weekend at the casino hotel, with amenities, courtesy of the casino's CEO. They planned when to leave. They planned which vehicle to drive. They planned what they should wear to the spa, on the gaming floor, and especially to the French restaurant.

Christmas Eve and Christmas Day would fall on a Wednesday and Thursday; their stay would be on the weekend between Christmas and New Year's. Smack in the middle of the holidays. What fun!

On Saturday afternoon, the women left the house at two for the hour drive to Capitol City in Minnie's Buick. Minnie had been chosen as the driver because she had already been to the casino and knew the road to get there. Three suitcases were tucked into the trunk; each woman also carried a huge tote bag. As the time when Minnie went to meet Rodney for dinner in his apartment, he would be waiting for them, this time at the hotel entryway; they could leave the car with the valet parking attendant who would assist with loading their luggage and other belongings onto a carry-cart.

Rodney gave the women time to get settled in the hotel suite and joined them in an hour to give them the access cards needed for the spa, pool, and other areas. For now, he had some responsibilities to attend to in the office but would meet them at the French restaurant at 7:00 p.m. Until then, they were welcome to enjoy whatever activities they liked.

None of the three women had ever been in a casino. They walked around, looking at the beautiful lighting and decorations. They marveled how clean it was. They said hello and spoke kindly to people pushing carts of soda drinks and water, offering them to the guests as they went. Finally, they happened on the gaming floor. Donna, being the more worldly woman of the group, had said many people saved their dimes and quarters in a special container and took them to the gaming floor to play. Ginnie, as a working woman who should be in the know, confirmed she had heard what Donna said from many people. But when they reached the gaming area, it was obvious the slot machines did not accept coins—paper money was the only thing they could use.

The women waited in the cashier line with several other people to exchange their coins for paper money. What to try first? Agreeing to meet in their hotel room at six to dress for dinner, each went her separate way. Donna and Ginnie went left and right to try their hand at some rollie things, but Minnie drifted toward an area of poker machines. She inserted a ten-dollar bill, read the instructions, and pushed the Deal button to register a one-quarter bet. If she remembered correctly, in the game of poker, a minimum of a pair was required to hold the hand. This game required at least a pair of jacks or two pair of lower-denomination cards to retain the quarter she had bet. She had been dealt a pair of nines. She pushed the Hold button to save the nines and then the Draw button. On the redeal, she drew another nine and watched her money total return to $10.25. She had gotten the original quarter she had bet in return, plus an additional quarter. Well, that seemed to be a winning situation.

She looked around at the other players and what she could see of their machines. One man was playing with five quarters, another with ten. She calculated the amount of money for ten quarters—$2.50 per bet. Even though the man seemed to be experienced at what he was doing, she noticed many hands he did not recover his original ten quarters. Minnie knew she did not know as much about casino gambling as most of the other guests; she decided to stay with a consistent bet of a single quarter.

When it was close to 6:00 p.m. and time for her to go back to the hotel room to dress for dinner, Minnie's ten dollars had become almost fifteen dollars. She had become familiar with the way the machine worked and refreshed the sequence of winning poker hands. It had been fun watching the numbers change on the video screen and sometimes holding her breath to see what would happen on the redeal. But right now, money meant so much to Minnie; she had learned how hard she had to work to save a single dollar. She needed to be careful how and when she spent money. She cashed out the slot machine, took the ticket to the cashier, put the ten-dollar and four one-dollar bills into her purse, and went to the hotel room to dress for dinner with Rodney and her friends.

CHAPTER 39

Dinner in the French restaurant was fabulous. Rodney complimented the ladies on their dress by saying other men in the casino were jealous of him because where they had no beautiful woman to accompany, he had three. He signaled to the host, and the four were seated immediately. The menu was in French. With a charming flair, as though he had been doing it all his life, Rodney ordered for everyone. Ginnie and Donna were impressed. Minnie wondered if he did this all the time to entertain guests and then, deciding she was being too harsh, admired his ability to learn the French language. She asked him when he had the opportunity to learn. He had spent two years in France after high school—on a junket, more like a vagabond traveling through Europe. He had an argument with his father and left the reservation. He put their disagreement aside when his mother became ill, and he needed to return home.

One more thing I did not know about you, Minnie thought. *Does this man have a story for every aspect of his life?*

After dessert, Ginnie and Donna hurried back to the gaming floor instead of going to the suite. Rodney asked Minnie if she would care to spend a few minutes with him in his apartment so they could talk privately. They rode the elevator to the third floor and walked past the exquisite paintings once again, arriving at his splendid rooms.

Once inside, Rodney took Minnie into his arms, saying as he held her how he had missed her, how happy he was she had consented to his invitation to spend the night in his casino, and how he wished he could have been able to spend part of the holidays with her. He explained how he had always made himself available to fill in on the work schedule during this time of year so other employees could take time to be with their families. He hoped Minnie understood.

They kissed fondly. He motioned her to the couch and went to the sideboard to pour them a glass of wine. After they had taken a few sips, he looked at her and said, "I've made a decision." He was going to step down from the CEO position after the Christmas and New Year holidays. His cousin, Grant Grey Cloud, was next in line to take over Rodney's job; he would be able to step in by the middle of January. Grant would need some guidance, but that would be part of the learning process.

Minnie happily received the news. She did not know Rodney's exact age, but she was sure he was at least five years, or more, her senior. He had taken on the position at a time when the casino was just starting. He had guided its operation through some difficult times and outside opposition. He had done his duty to his people. It was time for younger leaders with visionary ideas to have their chance.

Rodney wanted time to enjoy his ranch and his life. Now he would have it.

He's not so different from me, Minnie thought. *I worked to help George build his business. Now he is gone, I just want time to be me, put myself and my house back together after being betrayed by George, and enjoy life in the process. Do many people find themselves in this position at this age in life? And what would have become of Ginnie and me if we wouldn't have been able to start over?*

They finished their wine, and he took her back to her suite. No, she did not care to go back to the gaming floor. The spa was open until midnight, Rodney hinted; or they could relax in the swimming pool and hot tub for a few hours. He was through working for the day. What a good idea. "Get your swimsuit on, woman. I'll meet you there..."

CHAPTER 40

Minnie lay on the massage table, thoroughly enjoying the rub down the attendant was giving her. Oh, that made her old bones feel so good! She felt herself growing drowsy, and putting her head on her forearms folded in front of her, she gave in to the chance to relax.

She had risen early, dressed, and walked around the hotel and casino to see what Rodney called "his responsibility." Surprised to find the spa and massage area open so early, she remembered she had a free ticket and decided to treat herself.

While the masseuse smoothed away the kinks in her shoulders, Minnie closed her eyes and remembered the previous evening. She and Rodney had literally cooked themselves in the huge hot tub and then plunged into the colder water of the pool. What an exhilarating feeling that had been, so refreshing. They swam for a while and then did a few laps, finally settling on their towels next to the pool.

Later, when Rodney walked her back to the suite, she invited him in for a cup of coffee. But he had to refuse; he needed to turn in. He had to check in at the office at six o'clock. Still in the hallway, he took Minnie into his arms and kissed her more fervently than he had before.

Something happened.

It had been more than ten years since Minnie had felt any need to have sex. But there in the hallway, with Rodney holding and kissing her, both of them still in their swimsuits, his strong, male body so very close to her, more close to her than ever before—an urge awakened in Minnie she had not experienced for quite some time.

She wanted him! Lord, how she wanted him!

And Rodney, being a man, wanted her. He had made love to many women in his life, but making love had ceased to be something he attempted in the last few years. Not that he could not make love. Oh, he could! He had become more choosy.

But this woman, Rodney thought. This woman had lit a spark in him, as a man, he could not refuse. However, he would not give in to temptation standing here in the hotel hallway like a couple of hot teenagers. And he really had to leave. Carefully, he let Minnie go from his embrace, lovingly kissed her hand, and excused himself after saying good night.

When Minnie was safely inside the room, Rodney fairly sprinted back to his apartment. He had no intentions of embarrassing himself in the hotel hallway. He ducked into his bathroom, disrobed clumsily, and jumped into a cold shower as quick as he could.

In Minnie's hotel room, she tried to tell herself the warm feeling she had was a hot flash. She could not be reawakening sexually after being cold for so many years, could she? She could not be falling in love, could she? What was she doing? Her husband in his grave barely five months, and here she was carrying on with a man in the hotel hallway of a casino—in their swimsuits, no less. What would the country club gossip hounds have to say about that?

Well, if she was reawakening sexually, she was all for it. She had missed the closeness of making love. Mostly, she had missed the tenderness of the act George had displayed in the early years of their marriage. In their later years, it had become a sex act, not even close to being described as making love. A touch, a kiss, he would enter her and complete himself, not waiting for her to meet him in arousal—just, "Here I am. This is it. Then we're done." How much loving could a woman get from that? No wonder she shied away from him. There was no longer any mystery, any excitement in the act.

And this morning, Minnie thought as the masseuse finished, she awakened feeling exactly as she had last night. What did the kids call it? Turned on! She started to laugh out loud as she recognized the analogy. Yes, that is exactly what she was—turned on.

And now she was turned on she planned to enjoy it. To enjoy her new life. She showered, dressed, and went to the complimentary continental breakfast for the hotel guests with Ginnie and Donna.

CHAPTER 41

Barry Turner—Bear, for short—was not having a good day. He had spent his entire paycheck but for a hundred dollars. God, how was he going to exist for two weeks until his next paycheck on so little money? His whisky and beer habit each day would only stretch for two, possibly three days on that amount of money. Oh, man, he had to think of something. He desperately needed the booze. He needed it more than food or water—more than life itself.

As he dumped three or four aspirin into his palm, put them into his mouth, and washed them down with his first morning beer, a plan developed in his woozy brain. He would go to the casino and turn his one hundred dollars into more than enough money to reach for two weeks—or maybe even beyond that. He would hit a huge jackpot. Then he could quit his low-life job and live like a king for, oh, at least a month. Maybe even blow this iceberg town and head down south where the weather was warm. Yup! That was a plan.

He pulled on his dirty jeans from the day before along with the sweatshirt and his parka. Oh, good, the truck had just enough gas to get to the casino. No, he would not gas up; he needed the money to gamble. He could do it later, after he had won. He downed his second morning beer and threw the bottle onto the ground outside his dismal apartment building. There, let the caretaker pick it up; he'd had enough of this town—and its people, always cleaning, like the caretaker, like he was Mr. Clean or something.

Bear drank the third morning beer on the drive to the casino. One more and he would feel almost human enough to face the day.

He was just finishing his fourth morning beer as he reached the entryway to the casino when the Native American security guard stopped him at the door. The security guard said, "Sorry, sir, but bottles of alcohol or beer are not allowed on the casino floor."

"Okay, fine, I'll finish it here and throw the bottle away." With that, Bear flung the bottle into the shrubbery; it hit the nearby wall with a resounding crash. Oops! He grinned.

"Sir," the security guard had asked him, "how many beers have you had this morning?" Like it was his business to know! Bear politely told the security guard it was none of his business—at least, in his mind, he had been polite.

One more time, the security guard called him "sir." This time, it was while the guard suggested Bear leave the casino grounds. Like he wasn't good enough to gamble beside all the other rich people. Like he wasn't preee-cent-a-bull! Oh, now he was fighting mad. This was not how the plan worked. He had to get *inside* the casino to the slot machines to win the jackpot that would deliver him from this one-horse town to somewhere warm. *Just let me in*, Bear thought, *and I'll go away as soon as I win that jackpot.* He started to grapple with the security guard.

So many things happened at the same time:

As soon as Bear began arguing with the security guard, another guard alerted Rodney as well as the reservation police and the local Capitol City officers.

Sergeant Howell from the Bryant Hills Police Department and his wife had driven to Capitol City to treat themselves to the Sunday morning breakfast buffet at the casino. They had parked their car and were walking toward the casino entry.

Minnie, Ginnie, and Donna were walking around the gaming floor, doing a little "people watching" and admiring the huge, beautiful Christmas tree set up in the foyer of the entryway. Some of the bulbs were a foot in diameter.

Rodney responded to a walkie-talkie call from the security guard about a disturbance at the front door. An inebriated man was being denied entrance, and the incident was fast escalating into a fight. When Rodney reached the entryway and confronted Bear with,

"Can I be of any assistance?" Bear responded with, "Ho-o-o, Tonto! Yeah, sure, you can tell your braves here to let me into the casino."

Rodney had all he could muster to remain calm. He had not been spoken to so disrespectfully in a long time. Looking around, he quickly assessed the situation: a young man, already drunk this early in the morning; the broken beer bottle beside the wall in the shrubbery; the security guards, just doing their jobs. This man needed to be dispatched as quickly as possible—this was bad for business.

Bear continued to bad-mouth everyone around him, four-letter words streaming from his lips like water. When Minnie and her friends appeared at the scene and asked Rodney, "What's happening?" Bear bolted, standing straight, looking at the women.

"Ho-o-o, Tonto!" he said again. "Nice babe. A little old for my taste, but then your gray hair stands out, even if it is in a braid Indian style."

Rodney spoke quietly. "Sir, can we help you get home? I can arrange for you to be driven—"

"What?" Bear interrupted. "I don't want to go home. I just want to get inside and play a few slot machines, win some of the money back the White folks lost in the treaty." His voice was intentionally malicious.

"I'm sorry, sir, but you won't be going inside."

"Well, isn't that a fine kettle of fish. You Indians think you can tell us White folks where we can and can't go." Then eyeing Minnie and looking back to Rodney, Bear said with a surly tone, "Seems like you've got everything under control, Tonto, even a nice White b—"

Bear was so engrossed in what he was saying he did not see Rodney's fist coming at him. The fist hit him squarely in the nose, and wow, did it hurt! No one, but no one, hit Bear Turner without Bear Turner hitting back. Except, Bear couldn't get up; somehow, he had been knocked to the ground. Not by this old man?

The old man was looking down at Bear and saying, "Sir, my name is not Tonto. It is Rodney Grey Cloud, and this is *my* casino. And you, sir, are not going to go inside my casino today."

All Bear could think was, *Oh, crap, and now a squad car is pulling up the casino drive. Oh, crap! Damn, this is going to be a really bad day.* He so needed a beer.

CHAPTER 42

Everyone in the immediate vicinity of the casino entryway converged upon the scene. Sergeant Howell and his wife, the reservation police, the Capitol City police, gamers, and our three heroines. Bear Turner was helped off the ground. Rodney insisted Bear be arrested on a drunk and disorderly charge, and Bear, in turn, insisted Rodney be arrested on an assault charge.

Within minutes, the security guards cleared the area, encouraging everyone to have a pleasant day. When it was all over, Sergeant Howell stopped to talk with Minnie and the two other women. He introduced his wife. They all smiled at each other and said hello. When Howell asked Minnie how she knew the CEO of the casino, she explained they were here by his special invitation for the weekend.

Sergeant Howell's reaction was saying, "Mrs. Gardiner, I must say, you do show up at the most unusual places."

CHAPTER 43

Monday morning dawned very cold; the thermometer registered twenty below zero. Ginnie's car refused to start, and the time was already close to when she should clock in. Minnie offered to drive her to the newspaper while Donna called Triple A for assistance. After dropping Ginnie off at the newspaper office, Minnie took a few turns and stopped in front of the building where Blake did business. The door to his office was partially open, so she walked in.

Calling his name, Minnie heard grumbling sounds from the inside office. Blake was standing by his desk, unloading his briefcase. He had not heard Minnie calling and was surprised when she pushed the door open.

"Oh, Minnie, did we have an appointment this morning?" he asked.

"No. I was in the neighborhood and thought I'd stop by to see if you had time to check on the zoning ordinance for doing business from my house."

"Why? What kind of business are you doing from home?"

"You remember, before Christmas when we had coffee at the bakery? And I told you how we were crocheting and selling baby blankets online? Are there any zoning restrictions for such an enterprise in a residential area?"

"Frankly, Minnie, no, I don't remember. Besides, how detrimental could it be to your neighbors if you sold a few knitted baby blankets?" he said dismissively.

"Crocheted," she corrected him.

"Whatever. You know, I really don't have time for this today. I have clients with much bigger issues. You are so resourceful. Why don't you check with city hall yourself and ask about this?"

"Well, I suppose I could…"

"Yes, do that. I need to get to work." That was the end of the conversation. He was such a different man than Minnie had known—so curt, so rude, so short with her. Nothing like the Blake she knew who always had time for her and his other clients no matter how minimal their questions or needs.

Minnie backed out of the office and into the hallway. She felt the sting of tears in her eyes and wanted to get into her car before anyone noticed she was crying. Blake had never spoken to her so strongly. Had she done something to offend him? She knew he did not care for her seeing Rodney Grey Cloud, but they had been through that, hadn't they? That was said and done, wasn't it? Had he somehow learned she, Ginnie, and Donna had spent the weekend as Rodney's guests at the casino, learned about the disruption caused by the drunken young man, and blamed her for his disapproval of her actions? That was too, too out of line.

No, there was no reason to refuse to help her. He had distinctly told her he was always available for any help she would need. He felt he owed it to her because he had been unable to stop George from putting them all into ruin.

But this today, this was different. This was a Blake she did not know.

Minnie sat in her car with the heater blowing. She dried her tears and then, stubbornly, put her head up, drove from the parking lot to city hall, and went inside. A directory was on the main wall of the entrance. Quickly, she located the office she sought and climbed one flight of stairs to find it. A pleasant-looking middle-aged woman wearing dark-rimmed glasses greeted her as she came in the door. She put her questions about zoning to the woman after explaining the new business she and her friends had begun.

The response was simple: no, a permit to operate a business within a residential district was not needed, provided customers were not coming and going from her home on a regular, daily basis. That many customers driving through a residential area would be considered a traffic hazard. But if this was not the case, if orders were accepted online, the payments collected through a system such as PayPal, and the items purchased were bagged and mailed from the post office, there could be no disruption of residential life.

The woman very helpfully gave Minnie a handout using red marker to indicate the area outlining this and other rules and regulations for residential areas of the city.

Minnie left city hall wondering if Blake already knew this information, and, if he did, why did he not tell her so when they were in the coffee shop? It seemed too simple. As a lawyer, he should have known this about his city. Why had he stalled? She remembered him saying he had forgotten about her questions. Why did he not just say so? Why such a pretense of getting coffee and Danish while taking copious notes?

She remembered how sick he had been the day after Christmas when she had called him. Perhaps some of the illness still lingered? Yes, that was it; he was not feeling up to par, had to work anyway, and had been irked at her appearing at his office without an appointment.

Minnie let go of the incident; it would all work out.

CHAPTER 44

When Minnie returned home from city hall, she was surprised to see Frank Jones in her kitchen drinking coffee with Donna. The two were visiting like old friends, while Donna continued crocheting a baby blanket. Minnie joined them. She wanted to know how Frank was getting along and what had happened at his court appearance.

Frank smiled broadly, stood up, spread out his arms, turned completely around, and said, "This, ladies, is a new man. For the first time in over twenty years, I am clean and sober. I had no money to pay the fines, but I sure could do the time. So, I did. Thirty days in the hospital in Capitol City. Thirty days with no alcohol to drink. Thirty days with counseling from a person who dubbed themselves as a 'recovering alcoholic,' a man who understood where I was coming from. Now I have a sponsor, and I am going to regular AA meetings. Like I said, I'm a new man."

Minnie did not know very much about the AA organization, but Donna did. She asked who had been Frank's sponsor. His old friend Sergeant Howell from the Bryant Hills Police Department, he answered. The good sergeant had been introduced to AA some ten years earlier, and this was a form of payback but paying it forward, showing someone else how to get the help they needed.

Frank remained silent for a moment before he began talking again. He needed a favor. He had a birthday since he had done time with the warden here; he was now old enough to collect Social Security. He had a position at the police station two days a week, doing janitorial work. What he needed was a place to live. And since Minnie had been so hospitable to him, he was here to ask if he could have his room back. This time, he could afford to give her a modest amount of rent each month. He could do odd jobs around here as well, he continued (like he had rehearsed the speech). There was firewood to be brought in for the fireplace, shoveling or sweeping the sidewalks and driveway to keep them clear of ice or snow, helping Leona with the cleaning two times a month…

Minnie began smiling as he spoke. "You don't have to tell me we need a man around this house, Frank," she said. "You can have your room back."

Frank said his backpack and other gear were stowed at the police station for now, he would bring them with after working the next day. He and Minnie agreed on the amount of rent he could afford, and the deal was sealed.

After he left, Minnie noticed Donna going through the house, smiling and singing. Minnie didn't know Donna could sing so beautifully.

CHAPTER 45

Minnie had tried to call Rodney several times since Sunday. She, Ginnie, and Donna had watched from the sidelines as the reservation police and the Capitol City police arrested Bear Turner and Rodney Grey Cloud. She hadn't cared much about the young man especially after the way he insulted her, but she was very concerned about Rodney. She knew Rodney could take care of himself; she would not compromise his pride by asking if he had hurt his hand in front of the crowd of onlookers at the casino. She would wait until they could talk privately.

Three days after the women had spent such a fun weekend at the hotel and casino and after Rodney and the drunken young man had been taken away by the police, Rodney returned Minnie's call. He was home, at his lodge. His phone had been taken away from him at the police station, and he was not able to return her calls until now. Could he see her? Would she mind driving out to his lodge? Did she remember the way?

Yes, yes, and yes, were Minnie's answers.

She told Donna she would be gone for a few hours and jumped into her car. When she arrived at Rodney's cabin, he was waiting for her outside, sitting on the steps. He looked tired, but he had had a chance to shower and change from the suit he was wearing on Sunday to a clean pair of jeans and a warm pullover sweater. To Minnie, he looked handsome.

Once inside the cabin, he put a mug of coffee into her hand, and they sat at the breakfast table in the kitchen as they talked. Due to Bear Turner pressing charges against him for assault, Rodney had to spend the night in jail, waiting for an appearance before a judge Monday morning. The unfortunate part was he had to share the cell with Turner. The drunken, surly young man had continued to badger him with disrespectful and profane language throughout the rest of the day until he finally passed out from the alcohol in his system. After that, Rodney made himself as comfortable as possible and waited out the time until he could talk to the judge. No, he was not hurt.

The judge listened to both men tell their stories. Turner had gone first, sounding pathetic as he talked about his menial job, low pay, and daily drinking habits. Turner just wanted to get somewhere warm and counted on winning a huge jackpot at the casino to deliver him there. The young man was still in the Capitol City jail because he did not have enough money to pay the fine for being drunk and disorderly. Rodney expected Turner would be released from jail to a facility where he could dry out and get some counseling. How Turner would be able to cover the court fines and subsequent charges, Rodney did not know.

Rodney was given a chance next to tell his story to the judge. He gave his position at the casino, what he and the security guards were attempting to do for Turner, and how the young man had reacted to them, and the surly remarks that were made about Native Americans and a female guest in the crowd. He felt the judge listened to what he had to say. The assault charge was dropped when Turner very loudly told the judge if he couldn't win a big jackpot at the casino, then suing "Mr. CEO here" might be just the ticket.

Clearly, the judge did not care for that remark. The judge did not take kindly to prisoners making threats against other prisoners in his courtroom. And this sounded too much like a threat.

Then Rodney mentioned Sergeant Howell from the Bryant Hills Police Department. Rodney was not aware Howell had been in the courtroom, sitting in the viewing area while he and Turner were appearing before the judge. After Turner's remark about suing Rodney, the judge motioned to Howell; Howell came forward. He and his wife had witnessed the entire incident, Howell told the judge. Everything happened as Mr. Grey Cloud stated. Although striking

Mr. Turner might not have been the best solution to the problem, Howell felt Mr. Grey Cloud was justified in his actions.

Case dismissed. Rodney was free to go home after paying a minimal fine. He had gotten a slap on the wrist!

Could anyone get a better witness than an officer from the neighboring town's police department? He owed Howell a ton of gratitude!

Rodney stopped talking and became very quiet. Minnie sensed he had more to say and needed a little time to put his thoughts in order.

"Min," he said as he looked at her, "can you forgive my atrocious behavior? This is not how I normally act. I don't go around punching people in their nose. I just couldn't listen to that drunken brat's surly remarks any longer. When he noticed you and I knew each other and he started to call you my White..."

He had to stop talking. He couldn't put the vulgar phrase into words. That was not who Minnie was. That was not what their relationship was.

"Min, I've fallen in love with you. You *must* know I want you. You have to know I care about you. I've waited a long time to have a woman in my life. When I met you, I had become someone who only had time for business, time for work. Then I began to know you and see the beautiful, caring woman you are. I dream about what our life together can be like. Don't you see? I can quit now. I can turn the casino over to Grant and remove this huge bail of stress from my back. Min, you like it here, at my lodge. Come and live with me. We can have such a nice life together—be together, every day. I love you."

Minnie felt her heart skip a beat. Saturday evening after they had returned from the pool, she would have jumped at the chance to make love with Rodney. She didn't feel different about him today than she had at that moment. She was just thinking more realistically.

"Dear, dear Rodney. How can I say this? I have the same feelings as you. I am so very fond of you, and, yes, I think I'm falling in love with you too."

"But what?" he asked.

"Well, we need to make sure this is the right thing to do," she answered.

"If we feel good about it, why shouldn't we do it? We're adults. We don't have to answer to anyone, not anymore."

"Yes, I agree. But we only just met. We've only known each other for a few months. Living together is a big deal. There are more people than just you and me to consider. You haven't had time to tell the council about your decision to turn the operation of the casino over to your cousin. I have people living in my house. It's my responsibility to take care of them. Rodney, too many other people depend on us. Oh, darling..."

He had not intended to make her cry. It was obvious she wanted the same things he did. It was obvious she had gone through so much turmoil over the last few months this was too distressing for her. She just couldn't see her way clear as to how to make it happen. He rose from the table, took her by the hand, and walked to the couch in front of the fireplace in the great room so they could be more comfortable. He sat close beside her and put his arms around her, cradling her in his embrace. He lowered his head to hers and kissed her softly. She kissed him back.

Tenderly, he lifted her and carried her to his bedroom. Putting her down onto his pillow, he lay down beside her. He reached for a windowpane from the end of the bed and lay it over the two of them. By the time Minnie stopped crying, she was snuggled warm against him.

Rodney looked at her face; she was not crying anymore. She was lying so close to him he could feel the curves of her body. His hand slid along the length of her, feeling her, purposely. His strong, warm hand slid underneath her sweater to her breasts, cupping her tenderly. One word of dissent and he would stop.

Instead, Minnie uttered, "Yes, Rod, I want you too."

CHAPTER 46

Later in the week, Minnie had another load of packaged blankets to drop off at the post office and mail. On the way home, she decided to stop at the local police station to talk with Sergeant Howell. She wanted to thank him for his attention to detail when testifying during Rodney's court appearance and for taking Frank Jones in hand and volunteering to be his sponsor for the Alcoholics Anonymous program. Howell greeted her warmly and jokingly said he was fresh out of prisoners for her to guard.

She asked him how Frank was working out at his new janitorial job. He replied the office area had never been so clean. Frank even took it upon himself to make sure the officers on the midnight shift had a fresh pot of coffee to get them through until morning. He also volunteered to run errands like picking up donuts and sandwiches when needed, sparing the time of an officer for more important tasks. When there was downtime in the office, Howell spent it training Frank to answer phones and handle some of the more minor office functions should the need arise for Frank to be in the office alone.

Howell knew Frank had asked Minnie if he could have his room back at her house and planned to pay her a modest amount from his paycheck and social security. Howell was glad Minnie had agreed. Right now, the more stability Frank had in his life, the easier it would be for him to stay sober.

They talked about a few of the upcoming events happening in the city, and Howell mentioned he was trying to contact Blake Harrison concerning the annual policemen's dance but had been unable to reach him. Knowing Harrison and Minnie were friends, he asked if she had spoken with Blake recently? Minnie sensed there was more to this than met the eye. She asked Howell why he was concerned.

Howell said he had heard something through the grapevine that was very disconcerting. Apparently, Blake represented a local man going through a divorce. The two had an appointment to meet in Blake's office. But when the man appeared for the appointment, Blake did not remember it. The man's court date for the divorce hearing was fast approaching, and he was so angered by the way Blake "forgot about him" he left the office and secured another attorney.

Howell hoped Blake had not forgotten about the policemen's dance as well. During a conversation at the bakery with an employee from city hall, Howell heard Blake Harrison had missed a couple of court appearances for two clients he was advising *pro bono*. Blake had literally left them out in the cold. No calls. No consultations. No response whatsoever.

Okay, now Minnie was worried about Blake. She remembered his rudeness toward her earlier in the week and had chalked it up to his being tired and run-down from his illness over the holidays. But this was different!

She told the sergeant about Blake's response when she asked his help to find out if she and her friends needed a permit to operate a business from her home. She told him how hurtful he had been to her, how rude, and how he could not remember they had initially discussed it over a cup of coffee. Blake had indicated he would have the information for her by the end of the day. But when she contacted him several times about the zoning ordinance, he was annoyed with her "simple, little" questions and told her to get the answer by herself.

Howell sat silent for a moment and even flagged Minnie not to speak as he continued to think. After a while, he told her she was right; this was not the Blake Harrison they both knew. Not the helpful man who gave freely of his time to anyone needing his expertise. Something was wrong, and not just being tired after an illness.

Howell knew Harrison saw the same doctor as he. Howell would contact her and see if he could get any feedback. If a wellness check was justified, Howell and the doctor would take care of it. Yes, he would keep Minnie in the loop!

CHAPTER 47

Ginnie offered Frank Jones a ride to and from his work at the police station. She was going his way and was sure he would appreciate it especially at the end of the day. February brought the customary far below-zero weather with an occasional snow flurry every day—just dreary enough for the townsfolk to dream about living in a warmer climate.

On his days off from cleaning the police station, Frank had done what he told Minnie he would do—bring in wood for the fireplace, make sure the sidewalks and driveway were clear of ice and snow, and help Leona with the every-other-week cleaning.

Last week, he had busied himself by pruning some of the apple trees and the plum tree. He explained to the ladies pruning would ensure healthier growth and tastier, bigger fruit from the trees. By the end of the summer, they would be able to see the difference.

At the end of February, going into March, the weather became warmer, and the temperatures reached into the forties. So pleasant and warm after the chilling cold. After taking a turn around the yard one morning, Frank asked Minnie to drive him to the local hardware store. He needed some supplies. On the way, he explained to Minnie what was needed: four large, ten-gallon drums, ten two-gallon-sized pails, spouts and spigots, a large aluminum-sided tray, two metal scoops, and twenty-four jars with lids and rings. He would order another load of wood when they returned home.

At home, Frank inserted the spouts and spigots into the maple trees surrounding Minnie's property. The pails were placed underneath the spigots. He positioned the drum close to the firepit in the backyard. When the delivery of a pickup load of wood arrived, it was stacked close to the firepit as well. Then he waited.

Drip, drip; slowly the sap from the maple trees dripped into the pails. When they were almost full, Frank emptied them into the drum and replaced them again on the spigots. By the following day, there was enough sap to begin boiling it over the wood fire.

For the next two weeks, Frank worked tirelessly emptying the pails of sap into the drum, cooking the sap in the huge metal tray over the wood fire. He would start early in the morning. As the sap cooked, it produced white foam atop the boiling substance. This was scooped off with the metal spoons. Approximately twenty-plus gallons of sap were cooked down to one or two gallons of golden maple syrup each day. After being removed from the wood fire, the syrup would be allowed to cool, and then strained through cheesecloth to remove any dirt, leaves, or other imperfections; and finally the syrup would be strained into the quart jars, covered and cooked in a canner to seal the lids.

The event was interesting to everyone living in the house and even to the young couple living next door. The pleasant weather pulled the people from their houses outside to the backyard. Rodney stopped by several times enjoying the chance to work outdoors and help Frank with a task that was native to his people. Rodney had been a lad of fifteen the last time he harvested sap from the maple trees. Under Frank and Rodney's guidance, the women helped with straining the syrup and canning the jars to seal. The group worked each day, visiting pleasantly around the firepit, telling stories, sometimes singing songs. At the end of each day, there would be several jars of syrup to show for their work, along with the feeling of a job well done. Evenings, everyone would go to bed, sleepy from being in the fresh air all day, eager for a chance to rest. The company and the task promoted an overall feeling of goodwill.

*****

During morning coffee one day, Donna asked, "Frank, what kind of business did you do before you started to have problems with drinking?" Frank did not take offense at the reference to his problem—his AA counselor had told him it was good therapy to talk about drinking; it was another way to understand himself.

Frank responded, "I was a gardener. For twenty years, I tended the grounds of a very rich gentleman living in Capitol City." He told his story to the ladies for the first time: he had grown up on a farm; livestock to care for, including milking cows twice a day; crops to plant in the spring and harvest in the fall; living in the fresh air, being his own boss appealed to him. When his parents passed away, he was to share the farm with his older brother. But the older brother did not want to be a farmer and sold his half of the farm without Frank knowing. Even though the new owner knew the purchase had been for half the farm, he moved his family and their belongings into the home where Frank had lived all his life. The new owner and his family were so obnoxious and made life so miserable for Frank he eventually sold his half of the farm to him as well but at a much cheaper price than his brother had received.

With a little money in his pocket, Frank wandered from here to there, searching for something he could do for the rest of his life. He always came back to some form of farming and gardening; and when he spied a position as gardener for the wealthy man in Capitol City, he grabbed it. He really liked that job! He even took a few evening classes in horticulture at the university to learn more about plants, trees, and such so he could do his job better.

Then the wealthy man died. His wife and children decided to sell the estate and move to a warmer climate. But, no, the new owner would not need a gardener; they already had someone else chosen for the job.

There he was, back on the street once again, right where he had started. He applied to several positions, but by then he was deemed "too old" for a company to take a chance on hiring him. He gave up. He could live off the county on a mere pittance and let all the fancy businessmen and women work their arse off while he could take enjoyment in his day, doing what he wanted. And by that time, what he wanted to do was to drink! It stung a little going down his throat, but it took away the pain of the life he had lost.

Yeah, sure. Except very soon he could not stretch the money from the county to cover his drinking habit for a month. Very soon, he discovered he did not enjoy sleeping in a doorway with newspaper blankets when the temperature ducked below zero. Very soon, he noticed more of his money was going for booze than for food. Sometimes, he would even trade his food for the booze.

He realized he could have a warmer and safer place to sleep when he would be picked up by the police and put into the drunk tank for a night. That wasn't too bad, until the night he was almost knifed by a man hopped up on booze and drugs at the same time. Then he started being more careful. He would earn a few bucks by helping clear trash and debris from the roads and highways in the spring and by raking leaves for homeowners in the fall. They paid him in cash. Cash was easier to work with when buying booze. This was what he had been doing when he was picked up the third time last fall on the drunk and disorderly charge. "Turns out, the third time was the charm!" he said, smiling. Sergeant Howell had no room for him in his jail, and he had landed here at this beautiful house with the warden and the two other women.

Sergeant Howell had also recommended Frank do the thirty days in a recovery facility and even told the judge he would personally vouch for him; Frank Jones would not be back in jail.

Quietly, he put his winter jacket back on and left to go outside and sweep the snow from the sidewalk. The three women did not speak; they all were thinking the same thing: "It takes all kinds of people to make the world go round. There, for the grace of God, go I."

CHAPTER 48

Donna Harper was doing well at her new teaching position. She began as a substitute instructor, working when other teachers had to take time off from their classes. She began the Monday following New Year's Day and literally jumped right in. Even though the students and teachers had just gone through the holidays with no classes, Donna was often called upon and usually worked every day. She made friends easily, and some of the older teachers in the Bryant Hills School District remembered her from her previous assignments.

What Donna liked most about this position was she could work from home, over her computer; most of her classes were taught online. Her students thought she was knowledgeable and patient. Junior high students could be rowdy, but in Donna's classes, they did not get the chance. They were not actually in a schoolroom—they were at home just like Donna. (And if she and her students didn't activate the video portion of the computer, she could teach in her pajamas!)

Donna thoroughly enjoyed working on a computer. Since selling the baby blankets had begun, she checked for new orders first thing every morning. This was another reason she liked teaching from home; she could more easily keep in touch with what was happening there.

This morning, following a breakfast of pancakes and sausages topped with their own scrumptious maple syrup, Donna was relaxing in the kitchen with a cup of tea while Frank poured over seed catalogs, a plate of freshly baked chocolate chip cookies between them on the table. Frank had convinced Minnie to let him broaden the garden area. The little "kitchen garden" she had cultivated was not big enough to feed the household, according to his standards. If the yield turned out to be too big, they could put some up in canning jars or freeze some, or if the vegetables were too overwhelming for the women, they could be taken downtown to the mission and donated for the street people supper. He was sure the mission organizers would appreciate the help.

He was making a list and talking out loud at the same time: onions, leaf lettuce, peas, green beans, zucchini, beets, squash, carrots, pumpkin, and corn. That should do for now. In spring, he would visit the local nursery and see what hothouse plants like tomatoes, cabbage, and kohlrabi were available to transplant.

Donna asked, "Just how big a garden are we talking about?"

"Oh, at least twice as big as there is now," Frank answered.

"Yes, I know, but do you have the footage? How long, how wide?"

"Not in the exact feet. Do I need to have that?"

"Well," Donna continued, "I was thinking of the squirrels and rabbits and other little critters."

"Let them get their own garden, and leave mine alone," Frank quipped, smiling broadly at his joke.

"Yes, I know," again replied the ever-logical Donna. "That's why I mentioned them. Shouldn't there be a fence around the garden or something to keep the little creatures out?"

What a great idea! "Warden, honey, you have a great mind," Frank said.

"Thank you," was Donna's response. "Now be sure to make measurements the next time you are out in the yard. You will want to be prepared with the exact amount of fencing you'll need when you tell Minnie about this."

"I'll measure right now," he said, rising and putting on his jacket.

Frank went out the back door of the kitchen and into the backyard. Some of the snowbanks had melted in the garden area so he should be able to walk off the number of feet needing to be fenced.

Donna watched from the kitchen window as Frank stamped purposely through the snow back and forth, and then back and forth again. She remembered the days when she was on the street. Even though she and Frank were on the street at the same time, they had never crossed paths. *I probably wouldn't have liked him if I came across him then,* she mused. *He would have been either drunk or hungover, on the verge of getting drunk again. I was always so afraid back then. Wow, both of us have come a long way since those days. Now here we are, in this beautiful house, all because of a caring woman like Minnie Gardiner. What would have become of us without her? And what was with this "Warden, honey"?*

Frank stomped the snow off his boots on the mat at the back door and entered with a cold rush of air. "Okay, I think I have it now. Approximately thirty-five feet wide and fifty feet long," he said as Donna wrote the dimensions onto a tablet.

"Great," she remarked, "that will be about a hundred seventy to a hundred seventy-five feet of fencing. And you will need to make sure it is high enough to deter our flying squirrels. They should be acrobats in the circus as high as they can leap."

"Is that all around the garden?" asked Frank.

"Of course," was her answer.

"All around the complete garden?" he asked her again.

"Yes." He could tell she was getting peeved with his question.

"Not gonna work," he said.

"You said thirty-five feet wide by fifty feet long. That is a hundred seventy feet in my book," was her curt reply. "Two widths at thirty-five for seventy, two lengths at fifty for one hundred. A hundred seventy for a fence to go all around the garden." *What was he thinking?*

"Not gonna work," he said again, beginning to laugh. Was there something here he was not telling her? "You should know. Gotta have a gate, you know, warden, honey, like a cell door. Gotta have a gate. Gotta get in the garden. Gotta get out of the garden. Otherwise, how you gonna pull the weeds?"

He picked up another cookie, blew her a kiss, jammed the whole cookie into his mouth, and went out of the kitchen, chuckling as he walked.

CHAPTER 49

Ginnie was so nervous she could barely key the computer. The editor, Jim Hall, had sent her an email late last night: Alistair Peabody would be in the office today around noon and wanted to talk to Ginnie. Yes, that was it—Alistair had asked specifically to talk with Ginnie. She was Ginnie. Alistair Peabody wanted to talk to her!

Alistair had been taken on to the newspaper staff as a "roaming reporter." He knew so much about traveling and the wonderful places to visit around the globe. He would have a column about travel twice weekly; he would also cover the "city" beat, talking about the events and celebrations around town. And he could pinch-hit as an editor if Jim wanted to take a vacation. They would be working side by side, every day. She, Virginia Gardiner, would be working next to the great Alistair Peabody, every day!

Ginnie wondered what he wanted to talk about. She hoped she would not do anything to embarrass herself while they talked. She so greatly admired him.

When Peabody entered the office, the usual flurry of activity came to a stop. He was such a likeable man everyone wanted to say hello and welcome him to Bryant Hills. He was a fine addition to its population. After a brief conversation with Jim, Alistair knocked on Ginnie's office door and said, "Let's do lunch." They bundled up against the cold, walked out to his car, and drove to the diner down the street.

Hot roast turkey sandwiches with stuffing on the side was the special for the day. That sounded good to them, and after getting their coffee and cream, Alistair began talking. Such beautiful countryside, such a picturesque little town Bryant Hills was, he said; how did she, Ginnie, choose it for a place to live?

Ginnie said she was a native—born here, grew up here, lived here her whole life. Alistair envied her, he said. He had been born a wanderer, and when he became an adult, he had turned his wandering spirit into a working dream. A few years ago, he started to feel out of place from other men because he had no roots. He also had no wife or children to hold him down. Even so, a man needs roots. One day while talking with a friend in New York, the friend said, "If you want to live in the United States, Alistair, you should choose a town in the Midwest, the Upper Midwest. You have the best weather, the four seasons, a huge variety of professional sports teams, and the nicest people in the country living right next to you. That was why he had come to Bryant Hills—to put down roots."

Ginnie listened as Alistair spoke. *He's lonely*, she thought. *He has traveled around the world, been everywhere, done everything, made many friends along the way, but he does not have a family of his own. He is a very lonely man.*

He asked about activities and events in Bryant Hills, and Ginnie talked as they ate. Now the holidays were behind them, things would slow down a little, waiting for the cold months to pass. But one of the annual events to take place was the Policeman's Dance in just a couple of weeks. Oh, Alistair sighed, how he loved to dance. (He pronounced it "dahhnce," with the *a* as "ahh.") And, oh, would Ginnie do him the honor of accompanying him to this dahhnce?

How could she refuse?

Over coffee, they did a little shop talk and then returned to the newspaper. Ginnie went to her office and Alistair into Jim's office for a brief orientation; he would begin his new job the following morning.

*****

Sergeant Howell was good at his word. He contacted his doctor at her clinic; she was with a patient now, the administrative assistant said, but if he would leave his name and number, the doctor would be sure to get the message and return his call. Howell waited impatiently at his desk, doing filing to take the edge off his nerves. When the doctor did return his call, Howell voiced his concerns about Blake Harrison's well-being. The doctor listened as Howell described the instances of forgetfulness Harrison was displaying and how detrimental this could be for his practice and career. Howell also mentioned Blake's illness over the holidays.

The doctor was reluctant to have Howell's officers do a wellness check. She had a much better idea, she said. It was not unusual for her to make house calls. She would visit Blake and see for herself if any of Howell's concerns were valid. This way, she would not have to divulge any patient confidentiality.

Howell agreed. Something was better than nothing. The doctor would have her assistant schedule a personal visit with Blake as soon as possible.

*****

She had not said no. That was right; she had not said no. That was good. And they had talked it through, for several hours in fact. Between making love. Oh yes, that was the best part. Rodney closed his eyes and could still smell her scent.

Rodney and Minnie had talked into the night, discussing their living together at his log cabin lodge. He would retire as CEO from the casino and provide minimal support to his cousin, Grant. Minnie would turn over operation of her house and property to her best friend and sister-in-law, Ginnie. They would live at his lodge, traveling when they wanted, loving each other, growing old together.

But just not yet. The agreement was for all those hopes and dreams when they had gotten to know each other better. Minnie was right—they had met only a few months before; they needed time to get to know more about each other. And in the meantime, there could still be the lovemaking. They were not children, not even teenagers. They were adults. And if making love and getting to know more about each other drew them closer over time, there would still be time to live together.

Minnie had stayed the night. When Rodney went back inside his lodge after seeing her to her car, he jumped so high he felt he could touch the ceiling.

*****

Bear Turner lay on his bed, staring at the ceiling. He had endured this place for almost thirty days; he could stand it for another five months. It was not difficult to do. On the second day here, he located someone who would slip him a little weed, enough to get through the night. Then he discovered the supply closet and made short work of breaking into it and confiscating a dozen bottles of medicinal alcohol. A half bottle of the stuff mixed with some water yielded a quart of hootch good enough to satisfy any hillbilly. And if needed, there was always the cute little babe in the women's dormitory he could hit for a quick lay. Yeah! He could make it through.

Bear was already planning what he would do when his six months were over. He would hunt down that old man who said he owned the casino and teach him a lesson like no Indian had learned. He would show the old man what happened to people who tangle with Bear Turner. Meanwhile, he had to beef up, Bear thought as he remembered how bad he had been hurt when the old man hit him. That was something else he could do to pass the time here—work out in the gym. And when he finished with the old man, he would look great for the ladies—oh yeah!

The plan he had made after Christmas had not worked very well. But this one would. Bear would make sure it would.

CHAPTER 50

Blake Harrison was doing something he seldom did—he was taking time off work. In the back of his mind, he knew there was a ton of paperwork waiting for him at his office; but he was so dizzy he thought it would be best if he did not drive to work; he could be a traffic hazard! Instead, he lay on the couch, a pillow tucked under his head, dressed in his suit and tie. He had made it that far, anyway. Well, he did have good intentions.

His phone rang. Blake looked around helplessly. What was that ringing? That was the sound of a phone, wasn't it? Whose? His? Where was his phone? By the time he located the phone (it was still on his nightstand where he had put it the night before when he went to bed), the ringing had stopped. With the alacrity of someone used to doing five things at one time, Blake located the voice messaging system and played it back: it had been his doctor's assistant, calling about an appointment. He could not remember if he had an appointment to see his doctor or not. He did not want to miss that!

He redialed the number and got the assistant on the line. What? Sure, he was at home now. Sure, the doctor could stop by, he was taking a day off, he would be here. He would have some lunch until she arrived.

Fifteen minutes later, his doctor rang the doorbell. As she came into the house, she smelled something burning. Blake did not know what it could be. The doctor took the liberty to go through the house. In the kitchen, she found a small kettle of soup boiling on the stove. But it was not just boiling. It was boiling over. And the handle of the kettle was so hot, even when she used a dishtowel to pick it up, she felt the intense heat through the terry cloth. She turned off the burner, took the kettle off the stove, and put it into the sink where no damage could be done.

Blake had stood watching her as she had entered his house, smelled something burning, and went to the kitchen to find the boiling kettle. He did not look alarmed, and he did not say a word. He looked as though he was looking through her.

The doctor walked around the kitchen, dining room, and living room of the home. It was in shambles. She asked Blake if he was going to work. No, he replied, not today; he was taking a sick day. She asked Blake if he was feeling unwell. Yes, he said. She asked him if he was hurting anywhere. No, he answered. He just felt fuzzy, like in a cloud; and he could not remember where he had put the papers he had been working on yesterday.

Remembering the information Sergeant Howell had passed along to her and how concerned Minerva Gardiner, a friend of Harrison's had been, the doctor did not call 911; she did not hesitate. She proposed Blake go with her for a ride in her car; perhaps some fresh air would help. Blake happily agreed.

As they drove through the streets of the small town, Blake anxiously looked around. At a stoplight, he suddenly quickly reached out and grabbed the dashboard. He gave her a confusing look and asked, "Do you know how to get home from here?" Remaining calm, the doctor replied, "Yes, Blake, I do." Her calmness calmed him. She refrained from asking him additional questions until they entered a long drive to a huge three-story building. "Wow," Blake exclaimed, "who lives here?"

She didn't have the heart to tell him it was a hospital. Instead she smiled at him like a good friend and walked with him to the emergency room entrance. She could call Sergeant Howell later. For now, she needed to care for her patient.

CHAPTER 51

Spring arrived at the end of March, and Frank was constantly putzing in the yard. With sweeping, raking, gathering sticks, and burning them and other debris that had gotten into the yard during the winter storms, he was always busy. The order he had placed from the seed catalog should be arriving soon. He needed to get the yard finished so he could start on the garden, had to get it tilled. Seed potatoes should be planted first, and soon.

Donna was working hard, too, teaching her online classes, attending virtual and in-person meetings with the other faculty, maintaining the website and spreadsheet for the crocheted blankets, and helping with the housework. Occasionally, on the warmer, sunshiny days, she would bring her laptop onto the patio. Donna watching Frank work, Frank watching Donna work. When he stopped and stepped onto the patio, Donna would quickly go into the kitchen and pull out a couple of sodas for them, which, they would enjoy, sitting in the sunshine on the patio.

She no longer called him "Mr. Jones." He was "Frank." He, however, persisted in calling her "Warden, honey." It was always said with a smile on his face. She had noticed the smile—it was very pleasant.

Today, they discussed the new boarder, Alistair Peabody. The travel writer had decided to settle in Bryant Hills after visiting and researching many small towns across the country. He began a position at the newspaper, working with Mr. Hall and Ginnie. When first moving to town, Alistair took a suite of rooms at the local hotel but, within a few weeks, decided to look for more "homey" surroundings. Ginnie had suggested the rooms on Frank's side of the upstairs. Alistair did not pause for a minute; he had accepted as soon as Ginnie stopped talking.

Frank said Alistair fell in love with Ginnie the first time he visited the city, or at least the first time he visited the newspaper, like when he applied for his position. Donna reasoned it could have been after he moved to the city and Alistair was working so closely with Ginnie every day. Either way, Donna said, she could see it too. Alistair idolized Ginnie; he was the kind of man who would kiss the ground on which his beloved walked. That sounded so corny to Frank he had to quit break and go back to work.

Donna put aside her computer for a moment and remembered the night Ginnie was dressing to go to the Policeman's Dance with Mr. Peabody in February. The woman was so nervous you would think she was sixteen and this was her first date. Then the jitters came on. Ginnie was having a bad-hair day. She had on too much makeup. Her shoes did not match her dress. "Enough!" Minnie had said. "You look beautiful. Now stop worrying. Everything will be all right, and you will have a great time. If you don't, you can always feign a headache, and Mr. Peabody will bring you home—he's that much of a gentleman."

Well, Donna was right about one thing. This was Ginnie's first date! Not many women are in their sixties before they experience their first date, but Ginnie was. The studious young girl working to get into a good college to become a writer had gone through her first year of college and then left college and landed her first position at the newspaper, eventually becoming editor of the "women's pages" without seeing many a man. She had meetings and appointments, worked side by side with men every day, and communicated with males of every level of importance or not. But she had never gone on what would "actually qualify as a date." No wonder she was nervous.

Slowly, little by little, Ginnie and Alistair became friends. When Ginnie arrived home each evening from the newspaper, it was, "Alistair did this," or "Alistair did that." She literally spouted information about what Alistair had done that day. Donna, Minnie, and Frank left her talk; they enjoyed seeing her happy.

And when Ginnie returned home one evening saying she had rented the last upstairs bedroom to Alistair Peabody, Minnie did not say a word. Minnie and Ginnie had been friends for life; this was Ginnie's home as well as Minnie's. There was more than enough room for another person in the household. Since Minnie was okay with the arrangement, Donna was too. Frank's response was simple; he was happy there was going to be another man in the house.

*****

Sergeant Howell phoned Minnie as soon as he hung up from talking with Blake Harrison's doctor. He had promised Minnie he would keep her in the loop. He invited her to stop by his office so they could talk. Minnie, knowing she would have to repeat everything Howell told her about Blake to Rodney, asked Rodney to accompany her to the Bryant Hills Police Station. Rodney, doing whatever he could to please the woman in his life, agreed. Now the three were sitting in Howell's office, drinking coffee as they spoke.

Harrison's doctor phoned last night as he was leaving the office, Howell said. She thanked him for his and Mrs. Gardiner's alertness to someone needing medical attention. She told Howell what she found at Blake's home and how quickly she had to act. Truly, she said, especially with regard to the boiling kettle of soup, she had arrived in the nick of time.

Harrison was currently at the Bryant Hills Hospital undergoing a series of tests to determine either dementia or the onset of Alzheimer's. He would not be going home soon. And he would not be going home at all until the doctor could employ two efficient male caretakers to attend to his personal needs—one for day care, one for night. At present, the doctor did not feel Blake should be alone.

In the meantime, the doctor wanted to know if there was someone either Howell or Mrs. Gardiner could recommend to organize files in Harrison's office, contact those clients, and inform them of Harrison's condition. Neither Howell nor Minnie had ever met any of Blake's lawyer friends. It was Grey Cloud who suggested the doctor contact the local prosecuting attorney's office to see if any of the junior members would be interested in the task. Howell thought this an excellent idea. After all, this was a job for an attorney, and an attorney would be able to ascertain if Blake's clients already had court appearances scheduled without breaking client confidentiality. Howell said he would give the doctor Rodney's suggestion.

Grey Cloud could see the concern in Minnie's face for her friend. She had known Harrison over ten years. During a span of time such as ten years, a person never thinks their friend will someday forget who they are, who other people are, where they are, or what they are doing. Minnie spoke of Blake to Rodney and Howell, lamenting his brilliant legal mind, his outgoing personality and helpful spirit. Alzheimer's is a disease through which you lose people twice, she said; you lose them when the disease completely takes over their mind, sinking them deeper and deeper into the unknown, and you lose them again when they pass away. How sad!

Minnie asked for the name of Blake's doctor and said she was going to call her to see if there was anything Minnie could do to help.

Yes, thought Rodney. Minnie would do that for a friend.

CHAPTER 52

The tribal council for matters relating to the casino was held every other month on the first Wednesday. Rodney had submitted his resignation in February, knowing it would generate a good deal of discussion. It was common knowledge Grant Grey Cloud would succeed Rodney as CEO of the casino operation. The question remained: Was he ready?

Since February, Grant began slowly taking over tasks Rodney had been doing for almost thirty years. An apartment like Rodney's was made available on the third floor to accommodate Grant. When the two men worked the same shift, they would spend a couple of hours going over spreadsheets, original documents, and procedures—especially procedures. Rodney knew his business so well he could talk for hours without notes or numbers to rely on; he knew them by heart. Grant developed a newfound respect for his older cousin. In turn, Rodney began to wonder why he had not shown Grant this part of the business before. Grant was an astute student, learning quickly and understanding why and how the business processes were done the way they were.

Grant was not a new employee of the casino. He had started at the bottom, working his way up the ladder so he knew how each position needed to be employed and supervised.

By the time the two men were ready to speak at the council at the beginning of April, Rodney was very hopeful the elders would approve the move for Grant to take over as CEO and Rodney could retire. Grant was eager to tell the council about a few of his ideas for expanding the operation. Rodney was careful to explain he was not stepping down because he was "too old" to run the business; he knew Grant had some good ideas and felt it was time for the operation to move on.

Their ancestors had a hand in swaying the council. Over many years, members of their tribe had depended on the good sense Rodney and Grant's grandfather and great-grandfather had when speaking to the council. The council listened to the pair now. They knew this time would arrive eventually. They had not expected it to happen so quickly. Time moves on, they said; they had not realized it was almost thirty years since they had named Rodney as the CEO.

Grant Grey Cloud was accepted as the new CEO of the casino with the contingency Rodney Grey Cloud would serve as a consultant and/or advisor for the next six months.

CHAPTER 53

Minnie entered the care facility and took the elevator to the fourth floor. She keyed in the access number to open the security door and stepped through to the pleasant sound of music. Someone was playing piano, others were singing, some were humming, and some were listening to the playing and singing with a wondering look on their faces as to what it was all about.

She noticed Blake sitting in a wheelchair at the outside of a circle. He looked at her curiously as she drew up a chair to sit beside him and took his hand in hers. Recognizing the words and melody of the song being played on the piano, Minnie joined in with the rest of the singers, mostly staff and family members of the patients. Blake continued to listen but did not participate in the singing. When the songs ended, Minnie rose and pushed Blake over to one of the tables at the side of the large room. She took a chair beside Blake.

She began speaking to him in quiet tones, continuing to hold his hand. She began by telling him who she was so he would not have a reason to be afraid of her. She talked about simple things that had happened at her house with Ginnie, Donna, Frank, and herself: what they were doing that day, what they had done the day before, what they were planning to do tomorrow. She talked about the weather. She talked about the young couple next door with their baby boy. Always, she spoke in quiet tones.

When she took a moment to catch her breath, Blake looked at her and said two words, "Grey Cloud."

"Not today," Minnie said.

She explained Rodney Grey Cloud was unable to accompany her to the facility today. He would come with her on the next visit. Although Blake did not respond well to Minnie's talk about what was happening at home, he enjoyed visiting with Rodney. Minnie thought this ironic considering how angry Blake had become last fall when he learned Minnie had gone to dinner with Rodney. Now Blake could listen for hours as the older man told stories of his life as a young Sioux brave and the adventures he and his cousins found. Rodney would stop occasionally to ask Blake a simple question, to which Blake would smile and nod but with no worded reply—just yes or no.

Blake had been diagnosed with advanced dementia at the beginning of the year. The dementia quickly became early stage Alzheimer's; and in less than six months, the disease took over what had once been a clever, friendly, vibrant, and caring man. The doctors could not find any reasons the disease attacked and screamed through Blake's body so quickly. From their experience, it usually took two to five years before dementia became a more difficult problem. But then they also saw cases where patients had Alzheimer's for over fifteen years before succumbing totally to the illness.

Yes, there were medications on the market to help deal with the symptoms. No, Blake's symptoms were too advanced for the new medications to be of any use. The most the doctors could recommend was to keep Blake safe and comfortable in the care facility. Daily and two or three weekly visits were recommended as well. Even with that, the doctors could not predict if he would, or would not, slip into oblivion.

Sergeant Howell had done as Rodney suggested and contacted the county attorney to see if there was anyone on staff who cared to go through Blake's client files, contact the clients, assist those clients with upcoming court dates, etc. There would be no salary, but the word was the attorney was not coming back to his practice due to a debilitating illness; any client fees from now on would go to whomever took over the cases. It was a quick way to acquire a practice for the right person. An unmarried woman, approaching middle age, jumped at the chance. She had been a social worker for the county while finishing her law degree and studying to pass the bar exam; she relished the opportunity to get her foot in the door of family law.

Meanwhile, here was Blake Harrison, in his early sixties, whose life and career had come to a screeching halt. Minnie knew, she just knew, the Alzheimer's would consume his mind and body quickly and before long there would be nothing left but a shell of the former man. She grieved for her friend. She grieved for the battle his body could not win. She tried to brace herself for the inevitable.

*****

When Minnie returned home that day from visiting Blake Harrison at the care center for Alzheimer's patients, she excused herself from the company of her household immediately after dinner and went to her room. She was feeling low. She turned the gas fireplace on, took a big afghan Ginnie had crocheted for her, and covered herself sitting in the sofa chair before the warm fire.

Minnie had never been a person who shared her feelings. She preferred to work them out by herself. In the earlier part of her marriage, she mentioned something to George a couple of times, and he berated her for speaking out. He told her she had the best of everything: big house, nice clothes, a husband who kept her in the style she was accustomed to. She had nothing to complain about! After that, she never voiced her dislikes to George again. It was obvious he did not understand.

But this was different. This time, her low feeling was not about her. It was about Blake Harrison. Ahh, now she recognized what was wrong. She was angry, angry at the circumstances leading to Blake being diagnosed with dementia and then to Alzheimer's.

And she was angry about something else too. *Someone else.* She was angry with God. Sitting in front of the gas fireplace, wrapped in an afghan, she was so angry with God she began to cry.

Why was he doing this? What reason could there possibly be to give a healthy, caring man like Blake Harrison this ailment? What could possibly be achieved from this? If the Lord was going to allow

Blake to succumb to dementia and Alzheimer's, what did he have planned for the other people in her life, including herself?

And what about all those undesirable people in the world? Why did God continue to allow the crooks to steal cars, sell drugs to children, assault women and children, and murder when they did not get what they wanted? Why didn't God give *them* this dementia? Give them this dementia and save the life of a good man.

Minnie was angry about other things too. She thought about Donna living on the streets after her husband had died and Frank becoming an alcoholic when his brother decided to sell his share of their parents' farm. She was almost thankful for the accident that had brought Donna into her life; she wondered what Sergeant Howell would have done if she had not made a place for Frank when the jail was too full. Certainly, the Lord did not have people like Minnie sitting around every corner, waiting to help someone!

She cried for Blake. She cried for Donna and Frank. She even cried a little bit for herself. Minnie had no answers to her multitude of questions. But she did feel better for being at the right place, at the right time, at least for two people. She would continue to help when and where she could. As for Blake, she would make time to visit when she could and to bring Rodney as well.

It was after eleven o'clock when Ginnie softly knocked on Minnie's door, quietly went into her bedroom, turned the gas fireplace off, and covered Minnie with a quilt. Ginnie was not going to attempt to get Minnie into bed. Eventually, she would awaken and move there herself. She noticed the remnants of tears on Minnie's face. *Oh, this woman*, Ginnie thought, *she cares and worries about people too much.*

*****

Bear Turner was making progress with his plan. He was counting the days until he could leave the treatment facility; less than two months to go and he would be out of there. He worked out in the gym every chance he had. His body was lean and hard.

He had cut out the weed so he could be more alert in the gym. One time, he was not concentrating and dropped the dumbbells onto his chest because he had hit the drug too much the previous night. Oww! He did not know how much the dumbbells weighed, but whatever it was, they were too heavy to rest on him when he was so strung out.

The sweet little thing from the women's dormitory helped occupy his time a couple of times a week. Man did not live by exercise and food alone. This man, Bear, needed a bit more "sustenance." She was gone now, released from the facility last week. Oh, well, he could always find another woman. He needed to concentrate on getting ready to beat that old Injun at his own game.

Two items remained on his list. He needed wheels, and he had to find someone on the street who would sell him a rifle. He'd had to sell his beat-up old truck (to a junk dealer for a mere two hundred dollars) to help cover the fines from his drunk and disorderly charge. The rest he worked off in the rehabilitation facility; that was why he was in for six months—because he didn't have the ready funds like the old Indian. *Another injustice toward the White man*, Bear thought. The rifle would not be too difficult to find, and if necessary, he could always steal a truck. He wouldn't be needing it for long, just until he had a chance to teach that old man a lesson, and then he would blow this state; he was tired of it.

CHAPTER 54

Jim Hall had been a newspaper man his entire adult life. He remembered his first week of employment well and never tired of telling anyone who was interested to hear about it.

Sixteen years old that fall of 1963, Jim had been promoted from newspaper delivery boy to overseeing all the delivery boys in Bryant Hills. In his mind, he had made it to the big time! He would be paid a full dollar an hour for the extra work he needed to do besides delivering newspapers to his own customers. That would put his weekly pay somewhere between ten and fifteen dollars a week. Not many guys his age could claim that!

While waiting for the newspapers to arrive from the printshop that day in 1963, Jim began to hear snippets of conversation from the newsmen and women in the office: Shooting in Dallas. Yeah, dead. Kennedy. Mrs. Kennedy covered in blood. Johnson would take over.

The news of President John Kennedy's assassination spread like wildfire, and soon the word through the office about putting out a special edition that day trickled down to the newspaper delivery supervisor. The daily paper was finished at the printer. The typists and page setup people were called back to work to transform the AP (Associated Press) printouts into type. Copywriters, proofreaders, and page editors worked side by side with underlings such as Jim to get the special edition out as quickly as possible.

The only sounds were the whirr of the typesetting machine and the linotype. The typists had tears streaming down their faces as they gathered the first news reports coming from Dallas. The page editors and page setup laborers were stunned into silence by what they were reading—the death of their president. How could this happen in the United States of America?

Jim Hall had been a newspaper man for almost sixty years. Throughout that time, he had witnessed and written about many a calamity; but the first one, the death of John Kennedy would always remain in his mind as the worst event he ever covered. The twin towers coming down in New York on September 11, 2001, was the only disaster he ever compared to Kennedy's death.

This morning, Jim Hall planned to do something so far out of the ordinary he was nervous going to the office. He was going to offer the position of editor to two people, Virginia Gardiner and Alistair Peabody.

Jim wanted to retire. He and his wife had purchased a home on the lake almost ten years ago; but with the constant demands of leading a company that was the only news media (except for the television station) in Bryant Hills, he had found little time to enjoy the beautiful lake setting of their home. He wanted time to take the boat out, sit on the dock, and fish early in the morning. He wanted time, to take time.

When he began his life as a newspaper man in the early '60s, the typesetting, page setup, and practically the printing had to be done manually. Today, once the typist finished punching an article into the computer, all that remained was positioning it onto the page. Even pictures could be copied and pasted from the computer screen. Newspaper delivery boys still existed, but many more people preferred to read their news online. The newspaper business was not going to be phased out; technology had made it easier to produce the daily news.

Jim had worked with Ginnie many years; he welcomed the addition of Peabody to the office. He thought he knew who it would be.

CHAPTER 55

He loved this part of the day. Carrying a large basket and seeing the lush green plants spreading their bounty over the garden gave him a sense of accomplishment he had not known for many a year. This was his realm. This was how he could give back to the people who had taken the time to help him come back to life. This was his garden.

Frank Jones truly was a master gardener. And he had proven so this summer, working in the garden in the backyard of Minnie Gardiner's house. Using some of her small stash of savings, combined with Frank's green thumb and help from the friendly people at the hardware store and the nursery, his garden was a picture to behold, a masterpiece.

Corn and sunflowers standing well over six feet tall over-looked shrubs of green beans, garden lettuce, cucumber, zucchini, acorn squash, and pumpkin. Big Boy and Big Girl tomatoes hung from their fencing, bigger than baseballs. Growing underground, as though it was a secret, onions, beets, carrots, and potatoes were ready to be pulled up into daylight, surprising their beholders. Strawberry and raspberry plants were bedded at the far end of the garden where they could spread their wings and prosper next year. (Avid gardeners always looked forward to what they could harvest next year.)

The beautiful view spread past the garden. The apple and plum trees held fruit that looked good enough to eat while standing in the orchard. The flowers surrounding the patio area enticed bees to come and pluck their pollen for honey. And they smelled nice too. The grass always looked as though it had just been trimmed. The sidewalks and driveway were swept daily, inviting visitors. Even Minnie and Ginnie's cars were always kept clean and sparkling.

Yes, Frank had worked hard. This was his realm. This was where he blossomed as well as the plants, flowers, and trees. He had done well. And he had stayed sober now for nine months. In his mind, he could not have done it without the help of these women and his AA sponsor, Sergeant Howell. He owed them a debt of gratitude he could never pay back in dollars. So he had created this beautiful backyard scene for everyone to enjoy.

This morning as he picked the vegetables, he wondered what would be done with them. Donna and Minnie had canned green beans the day before, putting them into Ball pint jars and cooking them in a huge canner to seal. The cucumbers, fresh green onions, and zucchini complimented each meal. The corn was ready to be picked, and the two women were planning to preserve it as well. Very soon, there would be more than an abundance of fresh vegetables for their daily table. How much could four people eat?

When he brought the large basket overflowing with corn, zucchini, cucumber, and green beans, the women exclaimed as he came in the back door of the kitchen. Wow! All these beautiful vegetables. And more to come. Frank suggested he and Minnie take the excess fruit to the downtown mission. Minnie and Donna thought this an excellent idea. They had more than enough. Tomorrow would yield another full basket. They were happy to share their abundance with others.

Frank washed the vegetables and put them into a box. Minnie was ready. Frank carried the box to Minnie's car, and the two set off for the mission. Minnie talked as she drove. She felt so good about doing something for other people. She and the others in her house, including Frank, had worked so hard to make ends meet, to take care of themselves, to become independent of the people or agencies controlling their purse strings. Now they would be able to give back to their community. She thanked Frank for his selfless idea. This would put more than a little sunlight back into their lives.

When they arrived at the mission, Minnie was struck by how bleak the building looked from the outside. Saying nothing, she followed Frank as he carried the big box of vegetables into the kitchen. He knew several of the cooks and had a triumphant look on his face as he explained they were from his garden, he had grown and cultivated them himself, and he had been sober for the past nine months. He introduced Minnie to the group, giving her and the two other women in her household most of the credit for his sobriety.

The cooks were overwhelmed by the abundance of fresh vegetables they would be able to serve to the street people. They would be sure to tell everyone where they had come from and how Frank was staying sober. The street people needed to hear a success story. Both the food and the story would lift their spirits.

After leaving the mission, on the way home, Minnie expressed her feelings to Frank. She was so happy she had been able to do something to help him. She met him at a time in her life when she felt she had been betrayed by the person who should have been there to help. Helping Frank by giving him a place to live had helped her as well. Now by donating the vegetables to the mission, she was feeling another sort of satisfaction. Helping others always took away the pain of what she, particularly, had to contend with. Giving back made her feel good!

Minnie made sure Frank understood how grateful she was to him for all the work he did in her yard every day. She knew he enjoyed being outside, working in the fresh air, but he needed to know he was appreciated the same as Ginnie and Donna. She didn't want him to feel since he was the only man in the household, he was being taken for granted.

Frank thanked Minnie for her kind words and then reminded her soon he would not be the only man in the house. Alistair Peabody would be moving into the remaining bedroom of the house next week.

"Yes," replied Minnie. "Imagine, a celebrity living under our roof!"

CHAPTER 56

Alistair Peabody. Prizewinning journalist, traveler extraordinaire. British, with the accent to prove it. Suave. Debonair. Currently on the staff of the Bryant Hills local newspaper. And now a member of Minerva Gardiner's household.

On a very warm day in August, Alistair Peabody brought his carload of belongings to the large Tudor home to live. He had tired of living in a hotel room with inches to dress and move about. There was no space to write or work on his laptop. There was no space to relax. He needed a house to live in. He could well afford one of his own, but when Virginia Gardiner made the offer to occupy the remaining upstairs bedroom at her sister-in-law's large home, he could not resist. He had lived in houses while growing up in England, had rented houses when working abroad, and now yearned to live in a house again.

Growing up in the county of Cornwall in Great Britain, in the tiny Hamburg of St. Richard's Way, his childhood had been magical, to say the least. The only son of a father who taught at the local elementary school and a mother who wrote children's stories for profit for the local newspaper, Alistair always had an exciting experience creating itself in his mind. He shared these with his mates, and together they would act them out, slaying dragons as they went. It was totally acceptable when Alistair finished college, he not return to St. Richard's Way but that he chose to travel around the world instead, writing about what he saw and experienced to those who would listen.

Alistair was so creative when he turned his little cottage business into a weekly column in one of the most widely circulated newspapers in the country everyone eagerly awaited the description of his travels. When his reporting increased the newspaper's readers by the thousands, Alistair packed up his belongings and became a traveler with wanderlust in his eyes. He was so friendly, so easy to talk to. He made friends instantly and forever. He made friends all around the globe. He made friends for life.

This was the man who had moved to Bryant Hills to experience "a bit of life" in small town USA before going home to retire in Great Britain. And why Bryant Hills? Why not some other small town? They dotted the countryside of any of the fifty states. Why Bryant Hills?

The answer was simple. Her name was Virginia Gardiner. He had met and liked many women over the years. But Ms. Virginia Gardiner caught his eye and his ardor like no woman had ever done before. He had to stay in Bryant Hills, live here, live close to her, work close to her, spend part of his life with her. When Alistair Peabody met Virginia Gardiner, he was bitten by the lovebug, big-time!

She was smart, inquisitive, observant, and, oh-so beautiful. He was sure she was a little younger than he but not that young. She knew how to handle herself around newspaper men. She never took a backseat to anyone. She worked hard and did her work well. He loved the spark that came into her eyes when she was working on an article, an excitement she gave to the reader, a hint of more to come.

He enjoyed being around her, growing toxic from the passion and electricity she exuded to her peers for the work they did. And what he liked most was the way she did it: with a smile, a "Would you please," and a nod of her head when she had put a fellow worker onto the right track. This woman had chosen to work on a very-small-town newspaper when she could have been a superstar on the biggest paper in the country. She had chosen to stay in Bryant Hills because it was her home. This was where she lived.

And, Alistair thought, *if Virginia Gardiner can live and prosper in Bryant Hills, so can I.* And that was why Alistair Peabody—prizewinning journalist, world traveler—chose to settle in Bryant Hills. It was Ginnie's fault!

So today, Alistair Peabody was moving even closer to Virginia Gardiner. He was moving into a room in the very house where she lived.

*****

Jim Hall, being a very perceptive man, figured out Alistair Peabody fell hook, line and sinker for Ginnie Gardiner the first time Peabody set foot in the office of Hall's newspaper. He knew the award-winning journalist wanted to work and live in a small town in the United States before going home to retire in England. He had learned this from a mutual friend of his and Peabody during a trip to Capitol City a few weeks earlier. When he suggested there might be a place for another editor on his newspaper and Peabody should stop and visit, Jim had no idea this important man would fall so hard and so quick for the women's page editor. That was not the purpose of Peabody's visit to Bryant Hills, but it surely became his focus.

Within weeks, Peabody moved from the house he was renting in another state and took up residence in the local hotel. Now Hall had to create a position on his newspaper for a newcomer. An idea hit him—this would be a good time to retire. Yes, this was his chance. Time to say goodbye to all the work and leave it to a younger man who could handle the daily grind.

After Alistair settled in, Hall would make the proposition. He would make it to both Alistair and Ginnie. He knew Ginnie would jump at the chance and Alistair would dive in right after her. He expected the new owners of the Bryant Hills local newspaper to be Alistair Peabody and Virginia Gardiner.

And he was right.

*****

Five thirty in the morning. "Okay, I'm up. I'm dressed. Now, for a large, very large container of coffee, two big crème-filled donuts, my phone. Yeah, I'm ready."

Grey Cloud opened the huge front doors of his lodge, stepped out and down the steps carrying his morning provisions, and walked the path around the corner to the lake behind his lodge. Sitting on the dock, watching the sun rise in the early morning had been the first item on his to-do list when he retired. But it hadn't worked out that way; too many other responsibilities had interfered.

For the first few weeks, it had been necessary for Grey Cloud to shadow his cousin, Grant Grey Cloud, as he made his way around the casino property executing his responsibilities as the new CEO.

Rodney was careful to stand aside, looking over Grant's shoulder, remaining silent as the younger man talked with the gaming floor employees, the cashiers, the accountants, the hotel attendants, the Native American security officers on daily rounds overseeing all aspects of the business. Grant had to learn to stand on his feet and grow confident in his new position. Only when absolutely necessary would Rodney step in, carefully suggesting, "You may want to consider…," or "Would it be better to…," affording Grant the opportunity to make the decision.

Now, finally, Rodney had a few days off, and he jumped at the chance to do the activities he had only dreamt of for years.

He didn't want to miss sunrise. He had set the alarm for 5:00 a.m., chastising himself—he was a full-blooded Sioux; he should know what time the sun came up!

There was just enough early morning light to find his way to the lake. A slight haze covered the pond, the coolness of the water meeting the warmth of the air. It was cool out here. Good thing he had chosen a flannel shirt over his usual summer tee. Gazing in awe at the beauty of the lake, he snapped several photos of it with his mobile phone camera.

The dock came into view, and he walked the length of it out to the fishing bench. Once there, he sat down to enjoy the coffee and donuts, his camera at the ready as the day grew brighter and brighter.

A loon giggled to his right. *Snap!*

A walleye jumped from the water to catch a fly destined to be a morning snack. *Snap!*

The haze lifted, and the first streaks of daylight spread like a fan of gold upon the water. *Snap!*

Oh, he was so enjoying himself. He heard a soft whiney behind him and turned left to see two of the horses making their way from the barn to where the paddock grass met the water of the lake's edge. He caught them on camera as they gracefully lowered their heads for a morning drink of water. So beautiful!

Grey Cloud could have been the subject of a photo himself as he sat on the bench drinking coffee—a mature man dressed in jeans, flannel shirt, work boots, and a worn brown Stetson. He stayed there until midmorning, possibly even dozing for a while in the sun, as it warmed the day.

Minnie, he thought. *My Minnie, she must see this. I must share this with her. Soon.*

CHAPTER 57

Man, it felt good to be back on the street. What was the saying? Free, free at last! Our wayward friend Bear Turner had finally gotten free of the law and its idea of proper behavior, aka recovering from alcohol misuse and being a gentleman in public, which meant, no fighting. Bear was proud of himself for persevering and making it through the six months of incarceration the judge had handed him. He had withstood the jail time, faked his way through the counseling sessions (even conjuring up a few tears when working for pity), and was able to make a reliable contact to secure a weapon when he was once again on the outside.

Some good, trusting soul who had actually used the program to become successful in life had directed him to a sympathetic farmer needing an extra hand with his animals and fall chores. Bear had spent two months milking cows at the break of day and again in the evening, shoveling manure from the cow stanchions; dressing over one hundred chickens, ducks, and turkeys; and helping the farmer's old lady carry vegetables from her extensive garden and lifting huge pots of boiling water while canning and freezing the garden's bounty.

It had been a baptism of fire, acquainting Bear with real country life as he had never thought of it before. But he did it; he kept the goal in mind of being free to be the person he wanted to be. He knew, but would not admit it to anybody, the best part was the room and board while getting paid for working at the same time. His bunk area was always clean and neat, and the meals cooked by the farmer's wife were the best grub he'd had in a long time.

With hard labor behind him, Bear now had almost two thousand dollars in his pocket. And the first order of business was a rifle. He would need it to steal the car or truck necessary to take him to the old man's ranch. After he had bummed a ride to town, Bryant Hills, Bear found a pay phone (had to be the last one left in the city) and called his contact to arrange a time to meet and see the weapon that was available. That done, he settled down to a beer and a sandwich in a sleazy bar in the red-light district.

Ahh! The beer tasted so-o-o good. He was back. Yup, you can't keep a good man down—and you may be able to put Bear Turner out of commission for a little while, but sooner or later, Bear Turner would be back. He felt good. He had a plan.

A few weeks before being released from the drug rehabilitation center, Bear had come upon an old buddy from his high school drinking days. During their conversations, he had learned the old man was no longer in charge of the casino. Now there was a different, younger man in his place. The friend had given directions to the old man's ranch on the reservation between Bryant Hills and Capitol City. With a twinge of jealousy because an Indian should own so much more than he had ever had, Bear took notes for the drive. Later, he consoled himself about not being able to have as much as the Indian; it would not matter—the old man would not have much longer to enjoy it. The old man and his ranch would be gone.

Thirty minutes later, Bear's contact sat down beside him on the barstool. Bear bought him a beer. They drank together like old friends and then went out to the other man's truck to do the gun deal.

Bear was pumped. *Yeah, now for a vehicle. Let's get this plan rolling!*

CHAPTER 58

"What is that man doing now?" Donna asked herself as she worked at the kitchen sink. She was coring crab apples, preparing to cook them into applesauce and then to store in canning jars. Every other time she looked up and out the window in front of her, she saw Frank Jones making another trip to the apple orchard to pick another bushel from the trees.

Donna, Frank, Ginnie, and Alistair had risen early. Ginnie whipped a batch of pancakes together while Frank browned bacon beside her at the big stove. Alistair looked to the coffee, and Donna poured juice and set the table. Minnie would not be joining them this morning; she had said she was going to sleep in when she retired the previous evening.

After eating, Ginnie and Alistair rushed off to work, Frank had a day off from his custodial position at the police station, and Donna planned to make applesauce. The pair quickly cleared the kitchen table and stashed the dishes in the dishwasher. Then they went to the backyard to pick a bushel of crab apples for the sauce. Frank carried the basket into the kitchen for her, remarking, "Here you go, warden, honey. Enjoy yourself!" Then he went back outside to the shed by the orchard.

A short time later, Donna noticed a large delivery truck at the back of the lot. She watched as two men unloaded several boxes from it and carried them into the shed. After the truck drove away, she did not see Frank for quite a while. Then she noticed him carrying a large basket of apples into the small shed, then another, and still another. What was he up to now?

She must have been wondering out loud, because Minnie said, "Pardon me?" as she came into the kitchen in her bathrobe.

"Frank," Donna answered. "He had a delivery of several boxes this morning, put them into the shed back there, and now he's picking and carrying bushels of apples into the shed as well. I can't figure out what he's doing."

"Oh!" replied Minnie. "The equipment to make apple cider must have arrived. He's making apple cider, to sell at the farmers' market."

Donna looked at Minnie. The woman knew what was happening around her house even in her sleep. Minnie caught Donna's remarkable expression and smiled. Over coffee and a couple of cookies, Minnie explained Frank had asked to purchase the equipment a few weeks ago. It included a juicer, large glass vats to store the juice while it fermented into cider, bottling equipment, and a machine to seal the bottles, along with twenty-four two-quart bottles and caps. She guessed (correctly) Frank was so excited about receiving the machinery he had to get started making apple cider right away.

It was a sound idea. During the last few weeks, the bounty of the garden coupled with the apples ripening had created another avenue for the residents of Minnie's house to earn an extra dollar. The plums and crab apples became jam and jelly and applesauce. The larger apples were scrubbed until they shined and sold in bags of a dozen; they were tasty and good to eat and made excellent pie. The women and Frank had taken their products to the weekly Saturday morning farmers' market at the city hall's large parking lot. Ginnie joined them bringing some of the baby blankets and afghans she and the other two women had crocheted. They were pleasantly surprised when customers surrounded their tables, drooling over the fruit products like kids in a candy store. They picked up the afghans, cuddling them close, admiring their beautiful, vibrant blend of colors. And, of course, everyone knew someone who was having a baby.

Their products were perfect. It was fall, and the weather was turning cold. A pretty, warm afghan to cuddle into before the fireplace, with a slice of apple pie or an English Muffin with plum jam or apple jelly to enjoy at the same time presented a relaxing picture.

When Sergeant Howell and his wife appeared in front of Ginnie's table to purchase an afghan for Mrs. Howell's mother and some plum jam for her father, the ladies knew they had a hit.

The Howells stayed for a moment, asking as to the well-being of the ladies and Frank, even extending the courtesy to Minnie for Rodney Grey Cloud, and then went on their way. The farmers' market was not just a place to sell their products and make extra cash; it was a way for friends and neighbors to meet and visit as well.

Frank had noticed how hard the women had worked to transform the vegetables and fruits from the backyard into products people would want to buy. He had willingly helped with the work, carrying, lifting the heavy baskets and boxes when needed. He was thrilled when he saw how eagerly people bought the jam and jellies. He wanted to do more, and the excess apples remaining on the trees as the weather grew colder gave him the idea to make the apple cider. He researched how to make the cider and found a company online from where the equipment could be bought. Today, it had arrived.

Minnie told Donna about this as the two women cooked the crab apples into applesauce and put the sauce into pint jars. They prepared chicken sandwiches for lunch; and Donna took a plate of sandwiches, cookies, and a steaming mug of hot chocolate to Frank in the shed. Entering the shed, she looked in amazement. Frank had unpacked the boxes and set up the juicer to begin the process of making the cider. Baskets of apples sat everywhere, and in the middle of the organized confusion was Frank, happily feeding the apples into the juicer. The smile on his face spread farther when he saw Donna enter his domain. He stopped working, rose, and stepped toward her. He pulled a chair close to him and invited her to sit with him while he ate the lunch.

They spoke as he ate; he told her how much he admired her, her knowledge of computers and the ability to teach young men and women. She returned the favor by saying how his gardening skills had turned Minnie's backyard into a profitable, lush oasis. Carefully choosing her words, because she had no intention to offend him, she told him how she admired him for the way he worked at maintaining his sobriety. She knew he worked his program and attended AA meetings every chance he had.

Before Donna went back to the house, Frank looked deeply into her eyes, thanked her for bringing him lunch, and put a soft kiss on her lips. She kissed him back. She liked this man!

Once again, Minnie noticed Donna's smile after she'd been talking with Frank.

CHAPTER 59

Ginnie and Alistair knock-knocked on Jim Hall's office door on their way out at the end of the day. Jim was busily pounding on his keyboard, and they had to knock several times before getting his attention. "Time to go home, Jim," Ginnie said in a friendly tone. "Tomorrow is another day. Plenty of time to get done tomorrow what you haven't finished today."

"I know, just a few more lines, and this editorial will be finished," Jim answered. "You kids go home. I'll lock up and leave in a few more minutes." The couple said good night and went on their way. It had turned colder, and they were eager to get home to a warm house.

Jim was trying to put the events of the last week into perspective for his Sunday morning edition of his newspaper. Even though there were more subscribers online these days than those who received the paper product, he knew many of the local residents regularly read and agreed, or disagreed, with his editorials. Tonight, he was writing how important it was for those who had not taken the time to get a COVID-19 vaccination to do so as quickly as possible. Jim felt the resurgence of the pandemic was entirely due to those who stoutly refused to get the vaccine. It was their fault the nation was once again facing many months of wearing masks, staying at least six feet away from one another, and self-imposing quarantines within households to decrease the number of patients suffering from the disease and the number of deaths.

He felt it was their fault as strongly as he felt the previous president was responsible for the thousands of deaths from the disease late in 2019. That man had known the coronavirus was in the US, in New York City and on the eastern coast of the country at that time. But he had chosen to tell the American people it was, once again, "fake news;" something the Democrats had materialized to create panic in the people because he, the president, could not be trusted to tell the American people the truth. Can we have a loud "A-duh!"

But that was another matter, completely different from getting a vaccination for a deadly disease. *Just a few more lines and the editorial will be finished,* Jim thought. He rubbed his left arm, hoping the pain he'd felt for the last hour would go away. He had debated with himself if a word from him would inspire those who hadn't gotten the vaccine to think twice and…

Wow! That pain was getting worse. What could it be? Maybe after all these years working on a computer, he was getting carpel tunnel syndrome? There was so much to write about: the forest fires in the Boundary Waters, the smoke from the forest fires in Canada drifting south to the US and the smoke from the fires in California drifting northeast, the political unrest in Afghanistan. America always had to take care of the tired, the weak, the poor…

The pain was getting worse now, almost unbearable. Jim couldn't see the print on the screen of his laptop. He felt dizzy. Nauseous. Oh no, not that, not yet. This wasn't the way it was supposed to hap…

Jim Hall's head fell onto his laptop, and he lapsed into unconsciousness, the stroke taking over his body.

*****

Alistair and Ginnie were still in her bedroom, talking late into the night. It had become a habit for them to meet there after the rest of the household had gone to bed. Working so close together as they did, there were a myriad of things to discuss between themselves; and they didn't want to talk shop in front of other people. Once or twice (or more), they had spent the night together with Alistair discreetly tiptoeing back to his bedroom in the early morning. They had decided to see what Donna and Frank thought about switching bedrooms so Alistair and Ginnie would be on one side of the large upstairs, and Donna and Frank on the other. The segregated girls on one side and boys on the other just didn't work for adults. The exchange could easily be handled with a few trips back and forth across the hall. Minnie would understand.

When Ginnie's phone lit up with an incoming call, both newspaper people were startled. Who? At this hour? Ginnie answered the call and listened intently. Sergeant Howell was on the line. She quickly put the phone onto the speaker option so Alistair could also hear. "Jim Hall. In the hospital. Stroke. Thought you'd like to know. Mrs. Hall could use some support."

Immediately, they had their coats on and were out the door, on their way to the Bryant Hills Hospital.

CHAPTER 60

The sound in the newspaper office was deafening. Not panic but very loud. Everyone was talking at the same time. Ginnie and Alistair clapped their hands together several times, loudly, to get everyone's attention. Once achieved, Ginnie explained Jim Hall had been hospitalized late last night with a stroke. She and Alistair had been notified by Sergeant Howell of the Bryant Hills Police Department and had gone to the hospital so Mrs. Hall would not have to go through this emergency alone.

It was early this morning before they left the hospital. Ginnie and Alistair had gone home to shower and change clothes and have a bite of breakfast before opening the office for the day. They had not slept. They were tired. "So, please, keep your questions short and to the point."

Yes, the newspaper was going to continue to do business.

Yes, there was going to be an edition printed today.

Yes, the Sunday morning edition was going to be printed; Jim had already written the editorial.

No, she didn't see Mr. Hall returning to work anytime soon.

Yes, she and Alistair were well-equipped to handle publishing a newspaper.

"Okay, you all know your jobs. You've been putting out a daily edition of the paper for years. You can do it now. The only difference is you will now be working for Alistair and myself."

Ginnie's tone was so calming and reassuring the employees were soon back on track. They got down to work, as they had always done, and soon the office was humming with the sound of the worker bees responsible for the inside production of any business.

Ginnie and Alistair went into her office to have one more cup of coffee. They were living on caffeine and adrenaline at this point.

Upon reaching the hospital the previous evening, they were met by Sergeant Howell. He explained two of his officers in a cruiser were making a safety drive around town and discovered the newspaper office door open and lights on inside. Inspecting further, they found Jim Hall slumped unconscious over his laptop on his desk. The officers notified Howell, who called Mrs. Hall, and arranged for an ambulance and paramedics to transport Mr. Hall to the hospital. From the information he had received, Howell believed it was a stroke.

Ginnie and Alistair had remained with Mrs. Hall through the night. The couple had no children and no relatives living in Bryant Hills; the newspaper people were their family. Just after midnight, an intern came into the visiting area to inform Mrs. Hall her husband was being prepped for open heart surgery, Mr. Hall was stable and breathing normally, and his blood pressure was significantly under control. She and her friends were welcome to come with the intern to another area where they would be more comfortable while waiting during the surgery.

And so they had waited. The intern had explained the surgery in layman words as well as he could. From birth, our heart has a protective shield, a form of covering surrounding it. This shield protects the heart from sudden attacks, like hits, falls, or accidents. If the heart did not have this protection, human beings would not be as resilient creatures as they were. However, somewhere along the way, during Mr. Hall's life, he had sustained an injury that broke through the wall of the covering. This injury could have been anything, especially if Hall had been athletic in his youth. The injury caused the heart covering to cease expanding and contracting throughout the normal course of life. Instead, it would now grow like a hard shell over the heart. Eventually, it can no longer expand or contract. And that is what caused the stroke symptoms. The heart needs to expand. When it cannot, the blood pressure goes out of control.

The intern continued. It really was not a stroke, but this was as close as it gets. Due to Mr. Hall's age, the doctors recommended it was time to retire. In any event, he would be recovering from the surgery for the next six months.

The doctors came out of surgery in the wee hours of the morning, saying Hall was in recovery, doing fine, smiling, and asking for soup. Soup! Jim was hungry for soup! Those were the nicest words the three people waiting on him had heard.

CHAPTER 61

"Min, Min, come on. This is what I've been telling you about. Time to get up, get dressed, get out on the dock."

Rodney gently shook Minnie's shoulder, whispering softly to her to wake up. He had told her about the morning he spent on the fishing bench on the dock, watching the morning sun rise. He showed her the pictures he had taken. They were oh-so beautiful, especially the horses and the first streaks of daylight upon the lake.

The previous evening, they had gone to dinner and then drove back to his lodge instead of taking Minnie home. She was ready; she had packed a tote bag to put into Rodney's car before they left for dinner. Since that first time in spring when she had ended the evening by staying overnight, she now planned for the getaway. He was a caring, patient lover, and she enjoyed the chance to unwind. He had reawakened her to sex, and for that, she was thankful. She felt like a woman again!

It was still early when they reached the lodge after dinner. They were enjoying a glass of wine on the patio, watching the stars. She rose from her chair to reach the bottle sitting on the picnic table to refill her glass. He came up behind her and put both arms around her, playfully capturing her in an embrace. He kissed her at the crook of her neck, sending chills down her spine. Oh! He knew so well how to begin their journey to love. He took the wine bottle from her hand and set it back on the table. He kissed her so strongly she was swooning by the time he stopped. Taking her gently by the hand, he guided her back inside the lodge, into his bedroom. Carefully, he lay her down on the bed.

This was the part she enjoyed the most—when he undressed her. He didn't just take off her clothes. He did things one at a time. "Now this button," "Now this snap," "Let's pull your sweater over your head." He'd whisper in her ear, "I have to find you a pretty sweater that buttons in front. Then I can undress you easier." They would giggle like two naughty children experimenting with one another for the first time.

And he didn't just touch her momentarily before entering her. He made sure she was properly kissed wherever she was touched. By the time he entered her, she was writhing in agony for him to join their loins. He was so much a man, so virile as he filled her. Together, pulsing, they reached their climax.

They stayed together for a while after reaching their peak, holding each other close, listening to each other's heartbeat—just them, no one else, Minnie and Rodney. Content. Minnie had always heard sex for people over a certain age was unpleasant, hurtful, ordinary, dull. Not so, she would protest silently. Not with Rodney Grey Cloud. Slowly, they separated but still lay close to each other. It had become a habit for them to sleep close—Rodney with his arm around Minnie, she with her head on his chest. The first night, they had done this to keep warm. Now they wanted to be as close to each other for as long as possible. Finally, they slept.

With Rodney urging her to hurry, Minnie rose and dressed as quick as she could. She didn't want to miss this spectacular event Rodney had been talking about for weeks. He had described it so beautifully to her she was eager to share it with him. When she reached the front door, he handed her a container of coffee, her fall jacket, and her phone—she definitely would need the phone.

He held her hand as they walked the path to the lake with the first morning streaks of daylight coming over the horizon. "Hurry! Here, hold on to me. I'll make sure you get to the end of the dock safely." She marveled at his ability to know where he was going, even in the dark.

For the next two hours, the couple drank coffee, ate donuts, snapped glorious photos worthy of magazine publication, talked, whispered, enjoying the beauty of the sunrise on the lake.

Rodney walked toward the barn as they came up the path from the lake. "Let me help," Minnie said. "There must be something I can do." He found her an extra pair of Wellingtons. They were too large for her, but she put them on over her oxfords and was able to walk easier. He showed her where the watering tanks were in the meadow for the sheep. He drained the tanks and then set her to watch as they refilled with fresh water. She attended to the three watering tanks as he shoveled out the horse stalls and lay down fresh hay for bedding. They hooked arms as they walked back to the lodge together.

Minnie cooked a breakfast of sausage, eggs, and toast; and they sat in the window seat in the galley kitchen as they ate. Sipping cranberry juice, she noticed Rodney looking at her intently. "What?" she asked.

"So when are you going to answer my question?"

"Your question?"

"The one I asked you in spring. It's going into fall now, and I'm still waiting for an answer. When are you going to come and live with me, here at my lodge? We agreed to get to know each other better, spend some time together, see if we can live with each other, together. We've done that. When are you going to come and live with me, here at my lodge?"

His intensity took Minnie by surprise. He really wanted this. He really loved her. Yes, she loved him as well, but…

No, no buts this time. He had done what she asked. Where had the time gone? Six months had flown by like a flash. Neither of them would get any younger. He needed an answer—now.

Minnie went with her heart. "As soon as I can manage it, Rod," she answered, putting her hands across the table and taking his into hers. "I would love to live here with you."

Rodney had half expected her to find some reason she could not move in with him now, something to postpone the event for another time. He jumped up in excitement, pulling her from her seat, and waltzed around the kitchen, holding her in the air. "Whoo!" he called out again and again. They were both laughing when he put her down. But he didn't let go of her. He held her, leaned down, and kissed her so strongly Minnie thought she would faint. Good Lord, this man was romantic.

They spent the rest of the morning with a tablet between them, making plans—this to do, that to take care of. They settled on a completion date. Two weeks. Two weeks from today, Minnie would move into the lodge with Rodney.

CHAPTER 62

Jim Hall's recovery from his surgery was not going to be short and sweet. No, not by any means. He was looking at a pleasant several months sitting by the fire with his wife, with therapy two to three times a week, doing lots of reading, even watching television during the day—something he had not done in over fifty years. In a way, he was looking forward to the privacy with his wife. He *had* been planning to retire; he just hadn't planned on making the detour to the hospital first!

When Virginia Gardiner and Alistair Peabody called to set a time when they could come visit, Hall was not surprised. He had been expecting to hear from them. Alistair so correctly British and Ginnie in her best business suit arrived at his door promptly at 4:00 p.m. Friends like these two called for a couple of drinks; and they, Jim and his wife, visited pleasantly, talking about the new developments in the nation's capital, what was happening in Bryant Hills, even gossiping a little with the news Minerva Gardiner planned to move to Rodney Grey Cloud's lodge.

The doorbell rang, and Jim's wife ushered a man into the friendly setting. He was introduced as Jim's longtime friend and lawyer; the documents making today's transaction legal were in his briefcase. He was also a notary public, so he could seal the documents today, making them effective immediately. The five people got down to business. An hour later, the Bryant Hills newspaper belonged to Ginnie and Alistair. For a down payment amounting to half of each of their lifetime savings, Ginnie and Alistair now owned a business. Not just a business! No, sir, this investment culminated a dream they both had had individually throughout their lives, and now they were making it happen as a couple.

For, you see, they weren't just any couple. As of yesterday, they were now a married couple. Ginnie still had her maiden name, but the ring on her finger told everyone she was a married woman. And Alistair, well, he was so proud of the woman he had taken for a wife he literally puffed out his chest like a peacock.

But they had not told a soul of these new developments. Not yet, that is.

Until Mrs. Hall could not help but notice the sparkles coming from Ginnie's left hand as she accepted the drink to celebrate acquiring the newspaper. And then the truth was out; and everyone, even the Hall's lawyer, felt like celebrating.

Yesterday, Peabody explained he and Donna Harper agreed to switch bedrooms at Minnie's house so he and Ginnie could be on the same side of the hall. It took no time at all to accomplish. And while putting things away into the closet and drawers, he had gotten another great idea. "Why don't we get married?" he proposed to Ginnie. "Right now!"

So they had. There was no waiting period due to their ages and his nationality. They rushed to city hall, filed the paperwork for a marriage license, found a sympathetic judge, and committed the deed. Today, in addition to buying a newspaper, they were on their honeymoon. They planned to return to work tomorrow but would take time off to go South for a break to warmer weather sometime in winter.

The happy couple accepted congratulations from the others. Jim Hall beamed. He had known how this would turn out. He had known all along.

CHAPTER 63

Minnie pushed the buttons entering the code to the Alzheimer's floor at the treatment center where Blake Harrison now lived. Opening and closing the door safely was a crucial part of being trusted with the code. Alzheimer's patients could roam freely about the floor but could not be allowed to go onto other floors or out of the building without supervision. Getting outside, into high-traffic areas, they could wander away—some, never to be found. The system was not very pretty, but it worked.

She and Grey Cloud were on their weekly visit to their old friend. After securely closing the door behind them, they walked down the hall toward Blake's room. An attendant greeted them in the corridor. Blake was in the activity room, he said, taking part in crafts. That was good news; Blake was taking part in crafts and communicating with other people. This was progress.

The laughter coming from the activity area could be heard before they reached the room. Through the plate glass windows, they observed Blake Harrison, of late prominent lawyer in Bryant Hills specializing in family law, holding his left hand out, fingers spread, with the others laughing, including himself.

Apparently, the goal had been to take a piece of cut paper, apply glue to it, and fold the ends onto each other to make a small ball. Three or four small balls would make a paper chain to decorate a small Christmas tree. Somehow, the paper had become glued to one of Blake's fingers on his left hand instead. Also, apparently, he had attempted the exercise again, and another piece of paper ended the same way. Now the former lawyer had three pieces of paper stuck to his hand and he was wiggling his fingers, making the paper wobble as well, creating rounds of laughter among the other patients. The nurses and attendants were laughing with the patients. This is how it goes some days; with Alzheimer's, nothing is predictable.

When the nurse noticed Minnie and Rodney at the window, she helped Blake get his wheelchair out from the table and pushed him into the hall. Rodney took over, moving the wheelchair toward a large, sunny area down the corridor. It was called the "Play Room" but was a more pleasant place to sit and talk when someone came to visit their Alzheimer's patient. Rodney parked the wheelchair close to the window; he knew Blake enjoyed sitting in the sunshine. Rodney set the brake of the wheelchair and sat down on the nearby couch, close to Minnie.

Blake was comfortable in the setting. He knew these two people. He knew he could trust them to take care of him while he was away from the nurses and attendants. He liked to hear the stories Grey Cloud told of his Indian youth. Sometimes but only very occasionally, Blake would volunteer stories of his own. Usually, it was difficult to decipher what he was talking about; then again, his story made sense. His language skills had diminished to one, sometimes two-syllable words. The frustration of this once-knowledgeable lawyer was difficult to watch.

Today, Rodney told a story of he and his cousin Grant fishing in the lake near Rodney's home. He was just approaching the part where a large fish jumped off Grant's line, back into the water, when Blake put his hand on Rodney's forearm. Rodney stopped talking. "George," Blake said, looking at Minnie.

Neither Minnie nor Rodney spoke. They both wondered if Blake had mistaken Rodney for Minnie's late husband. They wanted to hear what Blake had to say, if he had more to say. Blake looked from Minnie to Rodney and then back again. "George." Then there was a pause. "No, think," Blake said. He looked again from Minnie to Rodney and back again. Then he uttered, "Rod," with another pause, "good."

After he finished speaking, Blake smiled at the couple sitting on the couch.

Minnie knew immediately what Blake was trying to say. Blake had been at Minnie's side those weeks after George had died, learning how George had lost their insurance, profits, and retirement while playing with a woman who only wanted to take advantage of an older man. It was Blake who had helped Minnie make early decisions to help herself and her sister-in-law, Ginnie, keep a roof over their heads and stay alive. Blake's counseling and sound advice had helped Minnie get back on her feet after her husband's death.

Blake had also seen, along with Minnie, that George was not the good man everyone thought he was.

There had been those few times Blake became jealous when Minnie had dinner with or saw Rodney. Now this was his way of telling her he approved of Rodney Grey Cloud. It was as though Blake was giving Minnie his blessing to continue her relationship with Rodney.

Blake Harrison had had one clear moment of lucidity, and he used it to tell Minnie he understood.

CHAPTER 64

"Remember, one day at a time," said Sergeant Howell.

"And," Frank Jones continued the repartee, "let go, and let God."

The two men said good night, and Frank stepped out of the policeman's car. Howell was not only Frank's sponsor to the Alcoholics Anonymous organization, he was Frank's ride as well. Ever since Frank had first accompanied Howell to the meeting in February, the pair attended together. To Frank's surprise, Howell had told him Frank was responsible for giving Howell as much moral support as Frank had received from him. When Frank had received his Six-Month pin, Howell had beamed as though he was a new father.

Due to the closeness of their activities, the pair had become good friends. Going to AA meetings, working in the same office space several times weekly (Frank as the custodian, Howell as the sergeant), and taking time to talk on a personal level when things slowed down for a few minutes in the small town police station, the two men found a comradery they both enjoyed.

As Frank walked along the sidewalk to the kitchen door of the huge Tudor home he shared with Donna, Minnie, and the others, he reflected on his life, as it was now. If only he could have found these friends earlier in his life. It truly had been his lucky day when those thieves tried to rob the Bryant Hills bank, making it impossible for him to stay in the local jail. He *had* to go to Minerva Gardiner's house until it was time for his court appearance. He *had* to meet Donna Harper in the bargain. He knew he was running out of chances as sure as a cat runs through nine lives. Only a fool would not recognize the chance of a lifetime when he met the women and was put into their custody.

He laughed now to himself. Such a pretty warden Donna made. Her beautiful face looking at him sternly as she found chores for him to do around the house and yard. He would have been able to find those chores himself. He wasn't a man who had never worked around a home. He knew how to take care of things. She needed to show who was in charge, and he needed to let her.

And Minnie. What was it she had said with such emphasis as though she was a strict teacher shaking her finger at him? Oh yes, "If I so much as smell alcohol on you, you will be out in the street…" He also remembered how the police officers chuckled to themselves as they left him with the women that day, as though Frank would discover the meaning of the word *discipline*. If they could have only known!

As he entered the kitchen door, Donna was waiting, sitting by the table pouring tea into two cups, the ever-present plate of fresh-baked cookies nearby. Welcoming him in, giving him a hug after he had removed his jacket, she was always there for him—never prying but gently waiting for Frank to tell her about his night.

Frank and Donna had found common ground. Yes, they were friends, but the friendship went further than that. They had recently become closer. Exchanging rooms with Alistair had been an idea straight from heaven, as far as Donna was concerned. She had been looking for something, some way to get closer to Frank. *Thank you, Alistair!* The adjoining bathroom between their rooms meant Frank could come into her room, or she into his, during the night without disturbing anyone else in the house. They relished in their new privacy. They felt as though their two bedrooms on the same side of the hall were like a private bedroom suite, just for them. And in reality, it was.

The pair flourished. While Frank indulged his gardening urge during the days when he didn't work at the police station, Donna taught online classes to junior high students and on-site classes at the high school, and attended staff meetings, both in person and viral. Donna's computer expertise had impressed the administrative staff of the school from the start, and she was becoming more valuable to them each day. She had recently substituted for the assistant principal when the woman went to another state for her daughter's wedding. Donna beamed from the praise the principal had given her for a job well done.

To Minnie, Donna had become a right-hand woman. Aside from keeping the entire household organized with a computer app they could access through their mobile phones, Minnie now managed her budget and bill-paying activities online too. Donna clearly gave Minnie more time to do the things she wanted to do—to live and enjoy her life in her own home.

The couple knew their efforts were appreciated. Every day, Minnie made sure she told them how much she depended on their help. They were going to miss her when she moved to Rodney Grey Cloud's lodge.

CHAPTER 65

Minnie stopped making a list. She was in her room, the master bedroom of her large Tudor house. For thirty years, it had been the room she shared with her husband, George. But George was gone now, and the room had become "her" room—just hers. Looking back, thinking back at everything that had happened over the last year, everything she and Ginnie had gone through (*weathered* was a better way to look at it), Minnie marveled at how she had grown. Grown not just as a woman but as a person too. A person who literally took charge of her own life and helped make the lives of others better along the way.

How did I get here? Well, this time, she knew how she had gotten to this point in her life.

There had been so many other times in her life when she wasn't able to answer the question. And, oh, how she could have used a shoulder to lean on during those times. When she and George were first married and she suddenly had to take care of a house and all the tasks it demanded as George, Ginnie and their mother went to work each day. When her father passed away. When she lost her mother as well. When she miscarried a second time and was home alone when it happened.

She had always been alone, she mused. *We all are. Even in a crowd of people, we are always alone. Alone, onto ourselves. We are the ones who take care of us. I am the one who takes care of me. No one else can do it, because I am the only one who knows what I need. That's just part of growing up, isn't it? Yes, taking care of oneself is a huge part of becoming an adult, becoming a grown up.*

Well, she'd certainly done quite a bit of growing during the last year. She hadn't been aware of how much she needed to change until now. Good Lord, what was her life a year ago? Going to the spa and the hair salon twice a week, spending summer days at the country club, not always playing golf but spending time with vacuous women, just like herself, complaining about their husbands, how they were always at work and never home, complaining about their difficult lives, oh, on and on. Was she really like that? "Yes," Minnie answered her own question. She had been exactly like that. Looking back, in retrospect, Minnie could now understand why George had grown tired of her and looked to a younger woman. Minnie had been the kind of woman who only thought about herself and the social existence around her.

Sure, she planned and cooked and entertained at the endless dinner parties she gave in her beautiful home. Sure, she did the obligatory charity stints. Sure, she was seen and heard by all the right people. But she left her very existence, her life, her household up to her husband to figure out as best he could. She never bothered to see what a bill amounted to; she just handed it to George and expected he would take care of it. If he had needed money bad enough to take a loan on her house without telling the bank he didn't own it, how many other times could there have been over the years when he needed help?

Minnie realized a man needed a woman to help him through certain times in his life, the same as a woman needs a man. And maybe more so; after all, she had made it through her life without breaking down or straying to another man. George didn't. Could it be, that big, strong man who had been an athlete in college wasn't as strong as she?

This time would be different, Minnie told herself. This time, she knew what she was getting into. This time, she was going into a relationship with her eyes wide open. Minnie and Rodney Grey Cloud had spent enough time together to know each other as well as they knew themselves. It hadn't begun with a sexual attraction; it had begun with friendship. It had grown into love. No walking in front of a person because she was better than he. No walking in back of a person because she needed to be subservient to him. Just walking beside this person because they took care of each other, leaned on each other when necessary. Together. With a person who cared for her as much as she cared for him. Together. That's what she wanted.

Minnie looked at her list. She wasn't taking all her possessions to Grey Cloud's lodge. Just her personal belongings: clothing and accessories; her desk and personal files; her big, comfortable sofa chair. A few items would stay in her house because her room would remain her room; there would be times when she would return and spend the night.

This afternoon, she needed a few things for overnight. Rodney had phoned earlier and invited her to dinner—one last night cooking on the grill before the winter weather came in earnest. They could spend the evening planning what to move on the following weekend.

Minnie rose from her sofa chair, put the list on her desk, and closed her overnight bag. She stopped in the sunroom, where Donna and Frank were watching television to say she would return in the morning. Then she got into her car and began the drive to the lodge.

CHAPTER 66

Stealing a set of wheels didn't turn out to be as easy as it looked on TV. Bear had his eye on a nice new extended cab pickup in the sales lot of one of the local dealerships in Bryant Hills. But the new vehicles operated with that keyless entry gizmo, and if you didn't have the remote fob to open the door, you were screwed. On top of that, the carmakers were now using a new design on the windows, so running a coat hanger down the side of the door to catch the lock to undo the door was getting more and more difficult.

His first attempt at stealing a car or truck was looking like a failure. And it was cold. And he was working without liquid motivation—in short, Bear needed a beer. He had some money. He could go to a bar, get a beer, warm up, have a sandwich along with another beer. That sounded like a good idea. That would give him time to think of some other way to get some wheels.

A burger with cheese, fries, and six or seven beers later, Bear felt like a man again. He had sat by the bar as he ate his lunch with his backpack concealing the rifle on the stool beside him. When an older man asked him to move the backpack so he could sit there, Bear was going to move somewhere else. But the guy was so friendly Bear decided to stay where he was. Especially when the man started talking about the Indians and the reservation nearby. And the more beers Bear bought for the old man, the more information Bear got. He learned the exact location of Rodney Grey Cloud's ranch half-way, or thereabout, between Bryant Hills and Capitol City. "Really?" asked Bear. "Sure," said the old man. "I can show you."

The glimmer of a new plan began to sparkle in Bear's brain. He offered ten bucks to the man for a ride out to Grey Cloud's ranch. He and Grey Cloud were old friends, he told his new bar buddy. Grey Cloud would be happy to see him. The man could drop Bear off at the end of the driveway. He would walk in to the lodge the rest of the way from the highway. He had been laid up for a while and would enjoy the exercise.

Off they went together—these two new, good friends.

The day had grown long by the time the old man driving his weary truck dropped Bear off at the turnoff in the road to Rodney Grey Cloud's ranch. After receiving the ten dollars from Bear, the old man sped back to town; now he had enough money to go back to the bar. Oh, boy, this was his lucky day!

The fresh, cold air hit Bear in the face as soon as he got out of the pickup. But that was good; he needed to think what to do next as he walked up the long drive to the old Indian's lodge. He stopped, pulled a sweater out of his backpack to put on underneath his light jacket, adjusted the rifle inside the tote, and continued walking.

The driveway to the lodge was quite long, more like a road instead of an entry to a place to live. Bear was happy he had the chance to beef up in the gym at the rehabilitation center. Yup, gotta be tough now. This is what he had been waiting for, for the last six or more months. Yeah, now he was going to make the old man pay for not letting Bear into the casino last winter.

Total darkness now. The lodge was about a mile in from the highway. By the time Bear reached the lodge and the outbuildings, he had formulated a plan. A Buick was parked in front of the lodge. As quietly as he could, Bear walked around the lodge looking in the windows. The same older White woman who had been talking with the old Indian at the casino last winter was inside now. And she looked like she was right at home being there too.

Except, Bear wanted Grey Cloud alone.

Bear had spotted a pickup in the yard. He could use it as a getaway vehicle after teaching the old man the lesson Bear had in store for him. An older vehicle would be easy to hotwire. There was a barn, with horses. That should be warm. He would wait there until the old Indian was alone.

He window-peeped at Rodney and Minnie as they ate dinner, cleaned up the dishes, sat in front of the huge stone fireplace and talked, and finally went into the master bedroom suite for the night. The longer he spied on the couple, the angrier Bear became. This old Indian had a better life than he did. This old Indian had a nice, okay, older White woman for his personal use. This old Indian could tell who could, and who could not, go into the casino. And he, Bear Turner, a White man, had no life at all. *Not fair! Not fair at all*, Bear thought. *I'll have to fix this.*

After Rodney and Minnie retired, Bear went to the barn and made himself comfortable in an empty horse stall. The old Indian's horses had a better place to sleep than he. With his rifle in the back-pack beside him, Bear slept a fitful sleep. There was so much anger pent up inside him. He would right everything in the morning. "You'll see! Just wait and see!"

CHAPTER 67

Sitting on the big brown leather couch in front of the fireplace at Rodney's lodge, after making dinner together, after clearing away the dishes, Rodney and Minnie were completely unaware of Bear Turner watching them from outside the windows on the patio. If they could have seen him, they would have thought he was crying. His expression was so forlorn they would have been wondering what was making him so sad.

Bear Turner was remembering his life as a young boy, when he still lived with his parents. There had been times when his parents had sat together on the couch, talking, smiling at each other, being close. Then at ten or twelve years old, he thought it was silly, how grown-ups found it necessary to spend lots of time being next to each other. Why in the world would a man want to hug a woman, kiss her? Eewwe! He remembered how irritated he was then by CindySue Baker as she tried to be near him whenever they had the same class.

But then CindySue Baker had her braces removed and became the cutest girl in junior high, and he was the boy she wanted for a friend, and life suddenly took on a whole different meaning for Barry Turner.

That was so long ago—before he was in high school and figured out how to jump-start cars, learned which old women were vulnerable to having their purse lifted as they came out of the grocery store (not the shoulder bag, the handbag; the other would be held too tight), and learned who to contact for just the right drug to put him into never-never land for the weekend. Bear could still see the anger in his father's eyes when he had been called by the local police and was in custody but not under arrest because he was still a minor. Not under arrest, then, but soon after his eighteenth birthday.

Once he became an adult, Bear discovered more fun vices—smoking, drinking, losing money at the casino. He found stealing a much easier way to get money than working at a real job. That was how it really had begun. Until one day, his father said, "Enough. You want to live like a gutter rat? Do it on your own time, not mine or your mother's. Get out…and don't let the door hit you in the behind."

Once Bear was on the street, there was no limit to his abilities to find the resources he needed to live. The world was here for his taking. He got along just fine. Sometimes, he would work at a job for pay, earning just enough to buy or get what he wanted; then he'd be off again, on to another adventure. Somehow, he had earned enough to buy his old truck, afford a sleeping room, have enough to eat. He'd get by.

It got harder when he started the whiskey and beer daily habit. A bottle of whiskey partnered with at least a twelve-pack of beer each day put him into hog heaven. But it was worth every penny. He could work for the money, usually sweeping floors or carrying garbage cans; but when his sticky fingers lifted a purse with the proceeds from some old woman's social security check, well, that was a special kind of thrill.

That's where Bear was the day last winter he decided to drive to the casino and gamble with his last one hundred dollars, win a big jackpot, and blow this rinky-dink town. Until Tonto—aka Mr. Rodney Grey Cloud, CEO of the casino—put a huge cog into his plans. The drunk and disorderly charge against him from the casino apparently held lots of weight with the judge, and Grey Cloud was personally responsible for Bear being thrown into that rehab center for six months. No doubt about it, Grey Cloud was responsible for making Bear's life miserable.

Before making himself a bed in one of the horse stalls in Grey Cloud's barn that night, Bear closed the huge back wall door. It hung from rollers and was easy to move. It made some noise but was nothing he felt he needed to be concerned about. The barn was at least five hundred feet from the lodge. Bear was still chilly from the long walk in from the highway to the ranch. He wanted to get warm, and it would help in the morning if the door was closed. He had a little surprise in store for Tonto. Tomorrow, Rodney Grey Cloud would pay.

As soon as the woman left in the morning. He didn't need to hurt any woman. Except when he was stealing purses from old women, Bear was always decent to them.

CHAPTER 68

The fireplace gave a soft, warm glow. Rodney had lit the fire before Minnie arrived at the lodge. Now they sat close together on the large brown leather couch, talking.

"Rod, have you had many women?" Minnie asked.

Grey Cloud shrugged and said, "Enough, maybe more than my share."

"Was there ever someone special?"

"Oh," he said softly. "There was. But that was a long time ago." He snuggled closer to her and kissed her hair.

"You told me you knew George was my husband when you came to buy his car. Tell me about her. I'll listen."

Remembering how he had Googled Minnie's background before he called the contact offering the Mercedes for sale, Rodney thought it's only fair. People their age have lived a lifetime before they meet someone else. Besides, he had been trying to think of how he could tell her about the only other woman in his life.

Rodney was very quiet for a long time. Slowly, softly, he began to speak. "Morning Star," he said. "Her name was Morning Star. I had come home from my wandering. My father had found me and told me of my mother's illness. So I came home, here, back to my parents' house, this lodge. My plan was to leave again after my mother had died. But afterward, my father was so distraught. He fell apart. He would do nothing for days on end. He would sit on the dock, staring at the lake for hours. Nothing to eat, no sleep. Just sit and stare. It was years later when I understood this was his way of grieving for her.

"I couldn't leave him like that. He was my father. He was the man who I had always been able to depend on while growing up. So tall, so strong, always knew the right thing to do. So patient when I would do something he did not like, taking the time to explain to me why there was a better way. So I stayed. He recovered, and we worked the ranch together. I took some classes at the college, and then I became interested in business administration and finished, earning my degree.

"It was at a college function where I first met Morning Star. She was so beautiful. I just had to meet her, find out who she was. We started dating, and it escalated very quickly into stealing away to make love. I was a young college student with a beautiful woman in my bed. Truly, I thought I was in heaven.

"Then, one morning, her father was at the door of our lodge, asking to talk to my father. In the Sioux culture, most of the decisions are made by the men. There's usually a woman who prompts the decision making, or is at the center of it, but the men settle it. Even though my father was a third chief, as my forefathers had been, he listened respectfully to what Morning Star's father had to say. Her father did not hold special status within the tribe, but he was her father. So my father listened to him.

"Morning Star's father did not trust me. He felt if I would leave my home after a disagreement with my father, how would I handle the stress of marriage. He felt that at some time in our married life I would leave Morning Star the same way I had left my home as a young man. He did not consider me good marriage material for his daughter and requested I not see her again.

"This was a formal request by a woman's father. I could say no, but the tribe would not look kindly upon me. I would have no honor. After my father died, I would take his place as third chief, and I could not do this without honor. So I stopped seeing her. Within a year, she married another man from our tribe. They moved to North Dakota. He was in the Air Force, and there is a large base close to Fargo."

"Did you ever see her again?" asked Minnie.

Another silence but not as long this time. "Yes, years later—by that time the council had asked me to participate in planning the casino business. They knew I had earned my degree in business administration, had lived and worked in the White man's world, and felt I had knowledge that could be helpful. I was flattered when they asked me to help. I never expected it would become my whole life.

"It's about twenty years ago now. I was attending a council meeting at the lodge of the second chief. We were on the patio because it was a beautiful spring day, and we wanted to enjoy the fresh air. The man had a large family—four sons and two daughters. But one of the daughters had become errant."

He saw the question in Minnie's eyes.

"An errant daughter," he explained, "is a woman who makes herself available to any man who wants her, usually for money."

"Oh," Minnie said softly. She understood.

"The daughter had returned unexpectedly to the home, and the second chief's wife was trying to get her to leave because she was an embarrassment to the family and because the council were there now, as guests in their home. Even though White men consider the Sioux as 'wild Indians,' there is quite a bit of propriety in our lives. The daughter had brought a friend with her. Word was the friend's husband had deserted her and the woman had become errant as well. The mother of the home was trying to get the two women to leave, but they would not. The uproar carried onto the patio, and when I looked at the two women, I saw Morning Star.

"Except she was not the woman I had known. She was no longer beautiful. Her face held a hardness I could not imagine. She was dressed in a bra and a pair of shorts cut so low you could see her buttock cheeks, like a woman who frequents bars, looking for men. I had to turn away. I could not look at her. I had to stay at the meeting and continue the business discussion. I left as soon as I could.

"I learned from a friend Morning Star had not been deserted by her husband. It was the other way round. She had left him. She had not only left him but left her two small children with him as well. She had been known to leave for days, sometime weeks at a time, leaving him alone to care for himself and their children. She left to be with other men. By the time she had nowhere else to go, she came home in disgrace, with nothing but the clothes on her back.

"I heard her father and one of her brothers drove to North Dakota to find her children. They were living with their father, very content, and, no, they would not return to their mother. By then the children were of an age they could decide for themselves, and their father did not want their mother back in their lives.

"For a while, I felt it was my fault what had happened to Morning Star. If I had not disagreed with my father and left to wander, her father would have been more accepting of me as a husband. I would have been able to make her happy to be a wife and mother, caring for her family. I would have been able to make her feel wanted and loved. But, in time, watching, learning about people and the things they do, I realized it was all out of my hands. I never had control of her. However, in some ways, I still consider her as a woman I lost."

A stillness came over the couple as they sat on the couch. They were so close Minnie could feel Rodney's heart beating. Quietly, Rodney whispered to her, "Thank you. I needed to tell you about her. You are the only person who would be able to understand."

Minnie hugged him and said, "Yes, Rod, you and me—we understand each other."

CHAPTER 69

As the couple were having coffee the following morning, Minnie noticed Rodney was very quiet. Too quiet. Perhaps, even melancholy from what he had told her the night before about his first love. Minnie had an idea.

"Come on," she said. "Let's bundle up, take our coffee, and sit on the fishing bench to watch the day warm up. Soon it will be winter, and the lake will be frozen, and then it will be too cold to do." That shook Rodney out of his solitude.

Quickly, they pulled their warm coats on, found hats and mittens, poured coffee into two containers, and set out for the lake. They didn't notice they were being watched.

There wasn't much to see this morning; the sun had already risen. The animals had all awakened earlier. Rodney commented as to why the horses hadn't come down to the lake for their early morning drink of water; but they might yet be on their way. From the fishing bench, the couple noticed voluminous clouds off to the west that, later in the day, could bring rain or sleet. They sat for almost an hour, arm in arm, close together, sipping coffee, talking about her move to the lodge the following weekend, until it was time for Minnie to leave.

Minnie quickly put her things together and into her car. She planned to see Rodney later in the day; he was coming to have dinner with her and her friends who lived in her home. After Minnie drove out of the yard, Rodney turned toward the barn to begin the morning chores. He would start with watering the sheep and feeding the horses first. As he walked…

"Hey, Tonto. Still hittin' on that nice White babe, I see. She hasn't grown tired of having an old man yet?"

Rodney knew who was talking to him immediately. But even more, as the fellow was talking, Rodney heard the unmistakable *click-clack* sound of a rifle being cocked and the shell loading into the chamber. He stopped, dead still, not even a twitch.

The only thing Rodney could think was, *Thank God Minnie had gone home early.*

The person holding the rifle wasn't thinking of any reason to thank God. He began firing the rifle, aimed at the toe-tips of Rodney's boots, making him step high to avoid the shots.

"That's right, Tonto," said the fellow again. "Show me how you can dance." A demented laugh and then, "Maybe you can do a war dance around the fire. Work up a little wampum." More laughter.

"What do you want?" Rodney asked of his intruder.

"Want? Oh, I want a lot of things. I'd like to have lots of money or land, like you. Or a place like this with some nice horses. Oh, Tonto, don't move." And another rifle shot went over the tips of Rodney's boots.

"I'm not moving," Rodney said. *What the hell! I thought this dirtball was in rehab.* What was he trying to prove by shooting at him? Did he not have a brain? Assault with a rifle or a gun; he's looking at serious jail time now.

"Is the old babe coming back?" Bear Turner asked. He really didn't want to hurt a woman if he could help it.

Rodney told him no. He was trying to move a little closer to the barn door. He thought the intruder was in the barn but could see the front door to the building was closed securely. He could be up in the hayloft. If Rodney could get closer to the barn door, then he would be out of the intruder's line of vision. That would give him time to unlatch the door and get inside the barn. The horses could give him some protection; he didn't believe the gunman would shoot at or near the horses. It was Rodney he meant to harm.

Rodney could hear the snorting and whinnies of the horses in the barn. *Why don't they go out the back of the barn down to the lake?* he wondered. They weren't hobbled. The backs of their stalls opened to the rolling back door. It was still open; he usually didn't close the barn completely until the first snow. They wouldn't make such noise if they were just hungry. There must be something else wrong. Rodney cared for his horses. It bothered him to hear them in such distress.

"Well," said the gunman, "I'm glad the old babe isn't coming back. I don't want to hurt her." His emphasis was on "her."

"But you sure want to hurt me," countered Grey Cloud.

"Oh, yes, Tonto," the gunman answered. "I'm going to hurt you."

Every time they had spoken to each other, Rodney had taken the chance to sidle a little to his right, closer to the barn.

"What do you intend to do to me?" Rodney asked.

"I'm going to burn you out."

Now, thought Rodney, and he jumped toward the side of the barn where he hoped he would be out of the line of sight of the gunman. He heard the fellow swear as he undid the latch on the front door of the barn, dove inside, and pulled the door closed behind him. A rifle shot shuffled the ground in front of the barn door, but by that time, Rodney was safe inside.

As soon as he was inside the barn, Rodney understood what the intruder meant when he said he was going to burn Rodney out. The unmistakable smell of gasoline permeated the building. Turner must have found the can of gas Rodney stored in the garage where the car was parked. He kept it for emergencies; living thirty miles between two towns could make for a long walk if the car or truck's gas tank were empty. The smell was extremely strong; the hay, the horse stalls, even the wooden beams of the structure must have been doused with gas.

And it was dark inside. Rodney realized what was annoying the horses. The smell of the fluid put fear into the horses' beings. And they couldn't back out of their stalls and run out into the paddock because the rolling back wall door of the barn had been closed. Clearly, this fellow had not just wandered onto Grey Cloud's ranch; he had been here for some time. Rodney bristled thinking Turner had been here while he and Minnie were together.

There wasn't much time to think of anything else as Rodney was thrown to the dirt floor of the barn by Turner as he attacked him. The two men had not been in close proximity to each other since last January, but it only took a moment for Rodney to notice his opponent was stronger than he had been. Bear, in turn, realized the Sioux had not weakened in strength. This thought was depressing to Bear; he always felt old people should be weak.

Bear had leaped from the hayloft above Rodney to pounce on him. The two men struggled to regain their footing as they grappled with each other. Bear, as the younger man, should have had the advantage. But Rodney held his own, getting a few good fist-falls into Bear's ribs and groin area. Once again, as in January, Bear was surprised at how hard the old man could hit. The hit to his groin left Bear writhing in the dirt.

Rodney took advantage of the hit to Bear's groin to run to the back of the barn and roll back the door opening onto the paddock. Furiously shouting to the horses to make them run, he herded them out of the back of the barn, down to the lake. He wanted them well away from the structure if this madman decided to light the gasoline sprinkled onto the hay and wooden stalls.

Bear Turner was ahead of Rodney Grey Cloud. While the former CEO was chasing his horses out of the barn, Bear took a book of matches from the pocket of his jeans, lit them two at a time, and threw them randomly into the hay in the stalls. He was so satisfied with what he was doing he failed to notice Grey Cloud coming at him full force. Just as he tried to say, "Whoa, Tonto," Turner again felt Rodney's strong fist coming into his jaw. *Oh, boy, that really hurt. Not again, Tonto. No, you don't get to hit me like that anymore.*

This time, Bear didn't stay on the ground as he had outside the casino door last winter. This time, Bear didn't stay down. He jumped to his feet and flung himself into the burning stall, sprawling with all his might onto Rodney. One more good hit and Bear would be free of him. With a madness he conjured from years of being alone and seeking revenge on Grey Cloud for all the abuse he'd had to take since leaving his parents' house, he violently smashed his fists into Rodney's rib cage until he heard something crack. The old man, cringing from the pain, lay still. Sensing he had beaten the old man into unconsciousness, Bear stopped hitting him. He'd beaten him; he'd won!

Bear took his chance. Laughing wildly, he ran from the burning barn.

Rodney Grey Cloud lay in the horse stall on the burning hay, motionless…

CHAPTER 70

Icy air poured into the barn from the open back wall. The warm glow on Rodney's back felt wonderful against the icy air on his face. He smelled burning hair. In an instant, he realized what was happening. He was lying on burning hay, and it had started the braid down his back on fire. Painfully, he brought himself to his knees, then to a standing position. Between his painful body and the smoke-filled barn, it was hard for him to breathe; the pain in his rib cage meant one or more of his ribs had been cracked or broken from the beating he had received at Bear Turner's hands.

Alerted by the heat on his back, Rodney reached back to grab his braid and, while doing so, pulled it free from the back of his head. Quickly, he threw the hank of hair onto the floor of the barn before it could burn his hand. He stomped on the braid to put it out of fire; there was more than enough burning already. He checked the rest of his body to determine if he was on fire anywhere else. No, not burning in any other place. Little lost. It was just hair; it would grow back.

Despite the flames coming from the burning horse stalls, Rodney stood still and took his mobile phone from the pocket of his jeans. It took less than thirty seconds to dial 911 to report a barn on fire and request police help to apprehend an assailant at his address. Yes, he had been injured. No, he couldn't stay on the line. Just send help as quickly as possible.

Rodney suddenly felt nauseous. He needed to lie down. He felt a desperate need to be in his lodge, where he could be safe until help arrived. He moved toward the front door of the barn only to discover it was latched from the outside. He had to go around the barn from the back to get to the yard and then to his lodge. Walking, half stumbling in pain across the yard, the only thing that kept him mobile and moving was knowing the comfort of his lodge, his home. Whatever could have possessed him so long ago to leave it to wander about the world?

It wasn't until he reached the six steps leading to the large double doors of the log cabin could he see they were both wide open.

Tiny plumes of smoke were beginning to come from the inside of his lodge.

Bear Turner was in his lodge, his house—not just burning his barn but burning his home too.

CHAPTER 71

Sergeant Howell wasn't just a policeman. Like so many other city employees in a small town the size of Bryant Hills, Howell did double duty. He was also a firefighter. When the 911 call came in for the fire department and the police department, Howell was on it like wallpaper on a wall.

Howell and Frank Jones were just sitting down to a break and a cup of coffee when the news of a fire and an assault at Rodney Grey Cloud's ranch, thirty miles out of the city reached them. Most of the other officers were on duty in cruisers, either on patrol or helping somewhere other than the station, or off duty for the day.

Frank immediately volunteered to watch the office and take incoming calls as Howell rushed to the other end of the police station to the hook and ladder area of the building. The 911 phone operator had already alerted firefighters and volunteers who were hurrying into their gear and jumping onto the firetruck as it stormed out of the garage.

There would be a problem but not so big it could not be handled. Residents in the area where this fire was located most often did not have fire hydrants available to hook onto the fire hose. This address however, had an option; there was a lake on the property. Knowing the address, the firefighters had loaded extra hose onto the truck before leaving the fire station.

The four vehicles made quite a parade as they sped along the highway to Rodney Grey Cloud's ranch: the police cruiser with two uniformed policemen inside, two hook and ladder trucks, each with four firefighters in the cab and at least four more hanging precariously from the handles along the side of the trucks, and the ambulance from the local hospital with two emergency medical technicians on board.

As Howell rode inside the cab of the firetruck, he took time to make two calls—one to alert Grant Grey Cloud what was happening at his cousin's ranch and the other to Frank Jones. He asked Frank to inform Minnie Gardiner as carefully as he could about the critical conditions happening at Rodney's ranch. She was *not* to drive to the ranch. It was now a fire and crime scene. Her being there would only be taken as interference by the other officers. She was being put on alert because Howell knew she and Grey Cloud were more than friends. She should wait until further notice from either Frank or himself.

With firetrucks honking their way along the road and police cruisers and the ambulance screaming their sirens for other drivers to "make way," the crew of first responders sped toward Rodney's ranch to help.

CHAPTER 72

When Grant Grey Cloud received the call from Sergeant Howell about a fire and an assault at his cousin, Rodney's ranch, the new CEO of the casino, dropped everything to help; he was a volunteer fireman on his reservation. As he was driving to his cousin's ranch, he contacted several other tribal members who would want to help too.

He had a shorter distance to travel than the first responders coming from Bryant Hills and expected to arrive before them. He had no idea what he would find there; his only concern was for his cousin's welfare.

*****

Minnie could not believe what she was hearing. Frank called her from the police station, saying there was a fire and had also been an assault at Rodney's ranch. Frank explained Sergeant Howell had cautioned her not to attempt to drive to the ranch; she would be interfering with the fire and police department's work. Frank agreed to keep her posted with any news he had as to what was happening. No, he had no idea how any of this had begun.

Minnie agreed to wait until Frank or Sergeant Howell contacted her about the incident. When she told Donna and Ginnie, who happened to be home from the newspaper today, both women vowed to stay with her until there was any news. Ginnie would be writing this story for the newspaper, and she needed to have firsthand information. She promptly phoned Alistair, apprised him of the situation, and said she would have the full story for him as it developed.

Donna—thankful Frank was safe, albeit holding down the fort at the police station—immediately put on another pot of coffee. It would be a long wait; they would need lots of coffee. Minnie talked nervously as she recalled what she and Rodney had done earlier that morning. Ginnie and Donna listened as Minnie told how she and Rodney had sat on the fishing bench overlooking the cold lake, peacefully drinking coffee, watching the animals, and making plans for her to move to the lodge in less than a week.

Minnie faltered a few times but quickly stopped talking as she felt herself breaking into tears. No! She would not become a bucket of mush. She would not let herself become a crying baby. She needed to remain strong. If for no other reason, for Rodney. She couldn't lose him now. *Oh, Lord*, she prayed to herself, *keep him safe.*

*****

Bear Turner had been busy since invading Rodney's ancestral home. He knew the layout of the log cabin because he had been stalking the couple the evening before. He already knew what he wanted to destroy and where those belongings were in the lodge. He half expected Grey Cloud to interrupt him while he was arranging his nefarious deed, but he still felt he was safe. He remembered the crack he heard when his last fist hit the old man in the rib cage. Naw, Tonto was down for the count. He had been beaten by Bear Turner.

Before anything, Bear wanted to destroy that brown leather couch. Using the poker from the fireplace tools, he jabbed holes in the seat and back cushions of the sofa. Then he used the small shovel to take still-warm coals from the hearth and dumped them into the rips he had made. He repeated the process with the rest of the upholstered furniture in the great room. He took an inordinate amount of pleasure from his actions and issued a snarly laugh. "Take that! And that!"

Pulling books from the corner library shelves added fuel to the fire, and soon there was just as nice a blaze coming from the burning furniture as there was in the barn. In no time, it spread to the hardwood floor and the drapes on the windows and French doors to the patio.

Gosh, he was good at building fires, he told himself. Too bad he couldn't find a job doing this all the time. Bear was having fun.

Now for that crazy-looking sword hanging over the fireplace mantel. It was made of wood—old wood, he noticed—so it should burn quick and well. Bear lifted the lance of Rodney's forefathers from its hooks between the stones from which the fireplace had been built over a hundred years ago. It was so old it would break up easily. Bear put it over his knee and started to exert pressure on the handle.

Rodney could not believe his eyes as he entered his lodge. This intruder, this cur, was holding his great-grandfather's lance over his knee—the lance Rodney had inherited when he became the third chief—and in the next moment would break it in half to burn like ordinary kindling.

"Stop!" Rodney shouted as loud as his injury would allow him to breathe.

Bear had not expected to hear another person's voice. He jumped not in fear but from being disturbed by someone, anyone, while he was concentrating so hard on breaking the lance. His annoyance turned to a hateful sneer as he saw who was addressing him.

"Tonto, you just don't know when to stay down, do you?" he said to Grey Cloud, literally spitting the words out of his mouth. "I didn't expect to see you walking around. I thought I'd hit you hard enough so you'd burn up with your barn. Damn, man! Now I have to beat you down all over again."

Bear had no idea of the rage going on inside Rodney's mind. All the dirty language thrown at him and his fellow tribesmen over the years; all the indignities the women of the tribe had to endure from men of other colors; all the degrading, demeaning stories about his countrymen—all of these abuses were embodied in the derisive language thrown at him from this fowl young man.

Throwing caution to the wind, ignoring his broken ribs, Rodney leaped onto Bear, spanning more than eight feet between them, like a cat leaps onto a mouse from a sitting position. By doing so, he caught the younger man unaware; and for the first time since

Bear had begun firing rifle shots at Rodney's boots, Rodney had the advantage.

Bear's arms flew from the lance to his sides in surprise. He had beaten this old man down, lying in a horse stall, a burning horse stall, not attempting to move with his injured rib cage. What the hell! What was this old guy trying to do, fight him all over again?

Before Bear could think of answers to his own questions, Rodney had delivered three quick *thwack, thwack, thwacks* to Bear's face, causing his nose to begin bleeding profusely. As tough as Bear thought he was, he did not like the sight of blood. It sickened him, brought on nausea, and made him afraid of his opponent for the first time since he had launched his assault against Rodney Grey Cloud. Okay, if the old man wanted to fight, they would fight.

Bear drew on all the strength he had acquired from working out in the gym at the rehab center, but he could tell by the furious hits to his body, especially his face and nose, the old man was his equal in strength as an adversary. Rodney's hits to Bear's body were relentless. Rodney did not plan to stop hitting Turner until one or the other of them were dead.

Bear Turner had done something he did not know anything about. He had invaded a man in the man's own home. And not just the man's home but his ancestral home. The home built for his family by his great-grandfather, his grandfather, father, all of their family from a long line of Grey Clouds. In addition to attacking a man in his own home, Bear had stated his purpose: he was going to burn Grey Cloud out. In other words, Bear was going to wage war against Grey Cloud the same as Grey Cloud would wage war on Bear Turner—until one or the other was done for.

Turner had never had this happen to him. Aside from being told by his father to leave his parents' home when he was a juvenile delinquent, Bear had never experienced anyone invading the place where he lived. Bear had no idea what he was dealing with. He had no idea of the fury he had awakened in Rodney Grey Cloud.

Furiously, relentlessly, the two men continued to lay blows on each other until Rodney backed Bear onto the burning brown leather couch. Grey Cloud fighting for his home, enraged beyond imagination at this upstart who had invaded his life; Bear fighting, well, just fighting at this point. Bear screamed when he felt the flames from the couch on his back.

Rodney left off throwing blows at the younger man for one second and straightened. As before, one second was all Bear needed. As soon as he felt Grey Cloud straighten his body from Bear's, Bear Turner escaped from the burning room.

CHAPTER 73

Turner had two avenues of escape when he fled from Grey Cloud's great room. He took the wrong one. If he had gone to his left, he could have been out of the burning lodge in an instant through the French doors and onto the patio. Unfortunately, he had gone to his right, pushing himself further into the burning building. Smoke as well as fire surrounded him, and he panicked, forgetting the floor plan.

Somehow, he reached the far wall connecting the second bedroom and the storage room. Yet again, he chose to go the wrong way. To the right would have led him to the open double doors of the entryway and outside into blessedly fresh air. Again, he had stumbled. Again, he took a wrong turn and went left, stumbling down the hallway, into another room.

But wait, this was the master bedroom. There were French doors from here leading out to the patio, just like the ones in the great room. Okay, he could go through them, leave them open, and wait to ambush Grey Cloud as he came after him. Oh, boy, would he have a surprise for him!

Rodney shook his head, trying to clear the smoke from his eyes. He knew Turner had escaped his hold once again. But this was his house; he would find the invader. Right now, the lance was more important. He stepped carefully around the area where Turner had been standing when Rodney had shouted to him. The lance was lying horizontally aligned with the fireplace, and when he stepped on the long shaft of the handle, Rodney almost lost his balance which would have flung him headlong into the hearth.

Recovering his position, Rodney grasped the lance and rubbed his hands over it to make sure it had not caught fire. It was safe! Knowing where he was inside his own home (better than Bear had taken notice of where *he* was) Grey Cloud moved to the patio French doors, opened them, and went out into the fresh air. He lovingly placed the lance of his forefathers on the picnic table, clear from the smoke and fire. Taking a few moments to clear his lungs from the smoke of his burning lodge, he put his hands on his knees and coughed the smoke from his body. Doing so, from the corner of his right eye, he spotted Bear Turner at the French doors of the master bedroom, squatting down, with his back toward Rodney, waiting… like a cat ready to pounce on a helpless little bird.

So that's where Turner had gotten to, he thought. Rodney knew Turner had gone farther into his house when he dodged from the burning couch. He must have gone down the hall to the bedroom and from there out onto the patio. From the way Turner was crouching, it looked as though he was waiting for Grey Cloud to come after him—to attack him once again as he followed Turner from the bedroom onto the patio.

Not this time, Rodney thought. *Now it's my turn to have the upper hand.* Quietly, Rodney crept over to the far end of the patio, approaching Turner from the back. Rodney lunged at the expectant ambusher, surprising him once again as to the old man's strength. Together, the pair grappled, this time more furiously than ever. They were both fighting—Grey Cloud fighting for his home, Turner because he was too stubborn to know when to quit.

They rolled, they stumbled, throwing blows at each other as they went. They traveled back through the French doors into the bedroom, down the hall, through the great room, and into the large entryway of the log cabin. Turner never stopped cursing; Grey Cloud winced and groaned from his injuries. On and on, they grappled until, at the entryway to his home, Rodney threw his fist with all the might he could muster into Bear's stomach. The blow sent Turner sprawling, rolling out of the big double doors of the entryway, down the six stone steps, and onto the dirt yard below.

Turner landed with a loud *Oomph!* This was getting to be too much. This old man was crazy. Bear never expected Grey Cloud to fight so hard to keep his ranch from burning. Bear always thought he would just go onto Grey Cloud's ranch, burn the barn and cabin, and leave the old man without a place to live. He never expected the old man would put up such a fight. Bear just thought he had a right to do this to the Indian because Grey Cloud *was* an Indian and *he* was Bear Turner.

What had happened? Now he was in a fight to the death with a crazy old man. In his zeal to make the old man pay for Bear's incarceration and time in rehab, Bear had underestimated him. He never planned on the old man fighting back as he had. Bleeding, bruised from the beating he was taking from the old man, Bear thought he should think twice and, maybe, quit while he was ahead.

He had no time to decide what to do. Lying in the dirt at the bottom of the steps, Bear Turner looked up and saw the most terrible creature he'd ever seen coming at him.

CHAPTER 74

First the police cruiser, then the two hook and ladder firetrucks, and then the ambulance, followed by another police cruiser that had joined the emergency crew drove into the yard of Rodney Grey Cloud's ranch. The burning buildings could be seen for miles from the highway. The firemen were jumping from the truck before it came to a full stop. Frantically, they assembled the additional hose needed to fight the blazes so it could be carried to the lake. The first police cruiser stopped just short of a bleeding man lying in the dirt immediately below the steps to the huge log cabin.

Sergeant Howell, in his firefighting gear, jumped from the first hook and ladder on the scene to take charge of the situation. The ambulance parked with the other rescue vehicles, the EMTs climbing down, opening the back doors to accommodate anyone who had been injured.

Something was happening. The young ruffian on the ground was screaming, apparently afraid of the older man next to him.

*****

After Rodney threw Bear Turner out of his lodge into the dirt yard, he felt an exhilarating feeling come over him. He could win this fight. He could win this fight against a younger, stronger man. No one had the right to come onto his land and burn his lodge. Not anyone.

The fury of Turner's attack and the heat of the fire had left him shirtless; after losing his long braid in the barn fire, the rest of his hair had come undone. He stood between the double doors at the entry to his lodge. With the flames of his burning lodge in the background and his hair streaming out around his head, he took a run and, with a shrill wild cry reminiscent of his ancestors, leaped from the top of the stairs, attacking his predator below.

Bear saw the vision pouncing down upon him, the battle cry reverberating all around. The attacker landed on top of him, and he had no defense. He could have sworn the vision was holding a tomahawk high in the air. "Oh, crap, oh, God, oh, crap! Please don't scalp me," Bear cried. "I'll go away and leave you alone. But please don't scalp me."

Scrambling out from underneath the vision, he turned screaming and running down the driveway, straight into the arms of Sergeant Howell and the waiting police officers.

Rodney saw the young man's reaction to his leap from the top of the steps. He stopped his war cry when he landed on the ground. As Turner scrambled out from under him, screaming and running away, Rodney could not hold back—ignoring his injuries again, he doubled up in laughter at the sight he had created.

Yeah! Take that from an old man.

CHAPTER 75

Running, screaming like a scared child straight into the arms of arresting officers had most definitely not been part of Bear Turner's plan. He had been handcuffed and arrested before he had a chance to calm down. Couldn't they see there was a wild Indian after him with a tomahawk, trying to scalp him? He had managed to burn Grey Cloud's barn and log cabin. He was supposed to be on the road to some state in a warmer climate right now. Didn't they know he was finally going to get that chance to have something nice for a change? Why were they arresting him when there was this other person running around wanting to commit bodily harm against him?

Rodney Grey Cloud—shirtless, shoulder-length hair frazzled around his head, and bleeding—had regained his composure. Approaching the officers, he announced, "Sergeant Howell, I want this man arrested. I'm charging him with aggravated assault, arson, and attempted murder."

The rifle was found in the dirt beneath the opening of the hayloft. It had Bear Turner's fingerprints on it everywhere. The burning buildings and the intense aroma of gasoline were evidence of arson. Bear Turner's fingerprints would also be found on Grey Cloud's can of gasoline. Rodney would agree to testify to the attempted murder charge.

Rodney watched as the prisoner received medical help before being hustled into the back of the police cruiser, driving to the Bryant Hills Police Station and a jail cell. While waiting for Bear to be seen by the EMTs, Rodney was heard to say to Sergeant Howell,

"And let's see what can be done to get this boy the kind of help he needs this time."

They ran the extra fire hose from the lake, and the blazes were extinguished swiftly. The barn was a complete loss. The lodge was uninhabitable. Grant Grey Cloud and his two brothers were on the scene as well and were busily rounding up the horses and herding the sheep into carriers to take them to his ranch until Rodney could make other arrangements for their care.

As the ambulance left the yard, turning on its siren for a fast trip to the hospital, Rodney, riding inside, took a last forlorn look at his beautiful ancestral home. Burnt! Burned to the ground! He and Minnie could no longer make plans to live their golden years here—not in a place that was burned to the ground.

CHAPTER 76

Minnie jumped to attention when her mobile phone started to ring. She almost dropped it when picking it up to answer. It was Frank. He gave her the most important news first: Rodney was okay and was being taken to the Bryant Hills hospital in the ambulance as they were speaking. Minnie began to cry in relief, despite her earlier promises to herself. Then came the rest of the report: both the barn and the lodge had burned. Some of the lodge was still standing, but no one could live in it at this time.

Minnie steeled herself. All those beautiful plans with Rodney—out the window. Gone!

She asked Frank how the fire had started. “Near as I can figure,” Frank reported, “it was arson. Sergeant Howell and the other officers are bringing a man back to the jail right now.”

After ending the call with Frank, Minnie fumbled into her winter coat, dropped her keys, stopped, and looked around the kitchen. Ginnie was on the spot. Retrieving the keys from the floor, she said, “I’ll drive. You have enough to think about.” With that, the two best friends, and sisters-in-law, were off to the hospital.

After an hour of sitting in the waiting room, the women were finally allowed to see Rodney. His body had been X-rayed from top to bottom, his broken and cracked ribs taped, and his bumps and bruises treated with care. He’d even been given an opportunity to comb his hair. Noticing this as she entered the room, Minnie asked what had happened to his hair. He quipped, “I decided it was time for a different look.” Minnie looked at him sternly, relented, kissed him softly, and said he had a lot of explaining to do.

"With nowhere to do it," again quipped Grey Cloud. "My lodge is gone. I have nowhere to go."

"Now you listen to me, Rodney Grey Cloud," Minnie said to him in a voice filled with concern. "You are coming home with me so I can take care of you, and I'll have no objections."

Grey Cloud turned a bleak look at the doctor. "What do I do now, Doc?"

"You do as the lady says, Mr. Grey Cloud. From what I can see, you are the luckiest man in the world."

Ginnie went ahead to bring the car around to the emergency room entrance. As Minnie helped Rodney walk out of the hospital and into the backseat of her Buick, Rodney remarked, "It's true, I have nowhere to go."

"Rod," said Minnie as she gently admonished him, "I have a house. My father bought it for me over thirty years ago. He bought it for me so I would always have a place to live."

CHAPTER 77

The first snowstorm of the season came on December first, putting a dusting onto the trees, buildings, sidewalks, and holiday decorations strung through the streets of Bryant Hills. It looked like a Christmas wonderland, straight from a Christmas card.

The residents in the large Tudor home had fallen into a routine typical of people their age. Well, not quite! Donna taught online and in-school classes; Ginnie, Alistair, and Frank reported for work every day; and Minnie and Rodney took care of everything happening at home. Minnie did the marketing, cooking, and general care around the house. Rodney was drawing plans—plans to rebuild the lodge at his ranch.

However, it wouldn't be a lodge where people could live. Not exactly. It would be bigger, accommodating meeting rooms, offices, a kitchen and dining area, a common room where the fireplace was, and about ten sleeping rooms. He was going to call it "Grey Cloud Lodge," for his forefathers. His cousin, Grant, was researching, finding people to employ for counseling, teaching, cooks, etc. He wanted it to be a special place for his fellow tribal members to congregate. The barn was also being rebuilt. The horses and sheep needed to be cared for daily. They would provide an income, wages for the people who took care of them.

He was drawing plans for community buildings. His family had lived by the lake, in the beautiful log cabin for over 150 years. Now he would share this peaceful scene with others.

Evenings in the large home were usually bustling with activity. The women cooked and served dinner, but twice weekly, the men took over. Meals from three different backgrounds made for a variety of food. When the men cooked, they always teased the women by saying they were broadening their horizons. Frank put it most succinctly, "You're never too old to learn."

After dinner was spent gathering round the huge fireplace in the living room. Playing board games, reading, crocheting, sometimes a little political debate—everyone believed in keeping their minds sharp.

Comradery! Peaceful, pleasant. Home. The huge, big Tudor home wasn't just Minnie's house anymore. It belonged to all of them. It was their home.

This night, they were excitedly looking forward to tomorrow. The following day was Saturday, and they had been invited to the home of the young couple living next door. Somehow, their little baby boy was turning one, and there was a party planned for Saturday afternoon.

When the adults arrived at the neighbor's house, they were surprised to see the baby was walking. Oh, boy, look out now, world. Barefoot, with his chubby little legs protruding from his diaper, the little boy was happy to show anyone watching what he had learned. Wobbling on his new legs, the baby walked precariously around the house, inspecting—and discovering—everything. When he stumbled and plopped down, he picked himself up, looked around, gave a huge smile to whoever was watching, and began his journey once again. It was clear he was very proud of himself for learning this new activity.

The group visited, talked, played with the baby, and drank gallons of hot chocolate until the young wife announced it was time for the birthday boy to eat his cake. Everyone gathered round the little boy in his highchair. His knowing mother had placed a bedsheet underneath the chair in anticipation of the baby's attempt at eating alone. Then she placed a huge cupcake in front of him. Chocolate cake with chocolate frosting—could a man ask for more? They sang "Happy Birthday." The little boy picked up the cupcake using both hands and took a huge bite. With a precocious smile, he took part of the cupcake apart with one hand and smashed it all over his face.

The crowd roared and clapped. It was Frank Jones who said, "That's right, just like a pro. You only get to be one, once. After that, the world is yours."

Going home, trudging through the snow, we see three couples: Donna and Frank, holding hands; Ginnie and Alistair, he with his arm protectively around her shoulders; and Minnie and Rodney, walking arm in arm.

"He's right, you know," Rodney said. "Frank is right."

"Yes," responded Alistair. "He is."

Ginnie put everything into perspective. "You are right, Frank. The world is ours. It belongs to all of us. It's what we do with it that makes a difference."

ABOUT THE AUTHOR

Abbi Weber believes you're never too old to follow your dreams. "I'm having the time of my life," she says, "the stories are pouring out of me." Weber incorporates her fifty-plus years of experience as an administrative assistant and her extensive family background into her writing. Mother, grandmother, and great-grandmother, she also enjoys her family, reading, crocheting, and playing cribbage and poker.

A Place to Live is her first novel.

CPSIA information can be obtained
at www.ICGtesting.com
Printed in the USA
BVHW080517061022
648789BV00001B/40